MARGIE'S GENTLE JOURNEY

MARGIE'S
GENTLE JOURNEY

A QUALICARE STORY

ANDREA NATHANSON, R.N.

Printed in Canada

First Printing, 2011

ISBN 987-0-9877763-0-3

Qualicare Franchise Corporation
3910 Bathurst Street, Suite 404
Toronto, Ontario M3H 5Z3

www.qualicare.com

FOR MARGIE'S GRANDCHILDREN

In my arms I caress you —
Each one of you, each time.
The burden disappears, and I begin to fly;
My soul takes off — Oh, how weightless! How pure!

And then I breathe again.
IN — OUT.
IN — OUT.
I am one with the air — I am my breath;
I am everywhere.
SMILE!
I am there.

Of my life, I only see my love.
I tried it, and I still feel it.
My arms open up; a great goodness rushes in.
It is the gift of love —
Oh, Oh my God! It descends upon me!
It descends in a burst of radiance — in a burst of light!
Love is the light; and I feel it is good.

One day, you will see this light — this burst.
It is as deep as the Earth, as wide as the sea, as bright as the sun,
And it engulfs me.
Oh God, it engulfs me; it guides me home.

ACKNOWLEDGEMENTS

I am deeply grateful to G-d for the opportunities He provides me to learn, grow and develop.

Margie's Gentle Journey is the result of the collaboration of phenomenal people who supported this project to ensure Margie's insightful messages and the important lessons I learned were communicated in a very real and meaningful way.

My editors, Marsha Zinberg and my nephew Oren Margolis were both phenomenal in bringing my original transcript to life so that the reader is captivated from start to finish. What a treat to work so closely with them both. They helped me create a masterpiece!

It is also vitally important to acknowledge the valuable service provided by The Temmy Latner Centre for Palliative Care. They enable many of our clients to remain in the comforts of their own homes while receiving compassionate and expert care. May you always have the resources to carry out this wonderful role so effectively.

My parents, Evelynne and Herb Loomer and my

mother-in-law Helen Nathanson are constants in our family. We feel so fortunate having you as role models in our life. My father-in-law Nardy Nathanson z"l, fought a courageous battle with ALS (Lou Gehrig's Disease). The lessons he taught me have become Qualicare's "heartbeat" since opening our doors in 2001. Nardy, you are forever with us.

My son Jesse, his wife Rivky, and my daughter Samara have supported the work I do from day one, even when I had to leave them for days to look after our clients. I feel very blessed to have their unwavering love, support and encouragement. Thank you, dear children.

My beloved soul mate and business partner Wayne is the ingredient in my life that fuels me to be the best person I can be. Our love grows stronger and stronger as we live life together. No words could ever adequately express my thanks to you.

Over the past ten years, we have been trusted to care for thousands of clients. To each of you, thank you for allowing us into your lives and for being the most incredible teachers. You are all my heros.

—Andrea

I am eternally grateful to *Margie* and the entire *Golden* family who accepted me into their lives and demonstrated to me what unconditional love and deep devotion to faith and family is truly all about. May her memory live on through those who knew and loved her.

—Andrea

PROLOGUE

ven now I see Margie before me. She is alive. She is smiling. Her luminescent eyes stare intensely at me, seeking reassurance, seeking honesty, seeking strength. She is gone now, overcome by the cancer that conquered her body but could not conquer her soul. Margie was so intense in her loving, in her caring, and in her stubbornness. Physically, she was slight, just over five feet tall, wiry and deeply tanned. A hiker and an adventurer, she exuded a zest for life that shone through her animated features. Despite her economic status, her home, her cottage, a successful, caring husband, three beautiful children and eleven grandchildren, Margie remained who she was — a down-to-earth, small-town girl determined to battle a mortal enemy head-to-head. As her caregiver, companion and confidante, I shared that battle, from her small victories, through her courageous struggle, to her brave, dignified death. I learned a lot about Margie. But

I learned even more about myself. Although relatively few people are professional caregivers, looking after loved ones is a duty that practically everyone has to face. Intentions are often to do so willingly; after all, consciously or otherwise, people generally realize that they too will be in a position of dependency some day. Unfortunately, the best-laid plans of families are frequently foiled by reality. Although the patient may try to focus on simply getting better, he or she is often sidetracked into stress and anxiety by the challenge of handling the care regime and the medical bureaucracy. Teams of doctors, nurses, physiotherapists, and nutritionists compete for the patient's attention, creating a situation that can be mind-boggling in complexity, and confusing in practice. Helpful family members despair at the lack of focus, and the inability of one single person to assume control over the entire situation. Their loved one is an individual; how can an individual maintain a level of personalized care within a system that all too often seems like an assembly line?

That's where I step in. I am the owner-operator of Qualicare, a Toronto-based healthcare coordination company that provides our clients with a revolutionary service aimed at advancing the patient's goals during a medical crisis. We are called upon to step into the breach that separates the healthcare system from the patient, liaising between the various service providers and articulating the wishes of the patient and family. I am a registered nurse by training, and have experienced firsthand the enormous disconnect that can exist between all parties, and which often stirs up an unhappy cocktail of frustration, confusion, and resentment. I believe that, above all, a patient's wishes must be assertively pursued. When the patient and family feel as though they cannot do so adequately, Qualicare case workers, myself included, can be called upon to serve as a single point of contact with the healthcare system, protecting the individuality of each and every case, and each and every patient. We strive to be courteous and considerate, resolute and effectual; in short, we are *nice*. Many think they know what this simple word means, but, truth be told, they don't. And I didn't either — until I met Marjorie Golden.

WINTER

ONE

My first meeting with Margie took place during the evening of January 24th. We discussed her illness, her upcoming surgery, and the role that I was to play in the whole process. But in truth, the meeting was hardly about any of those issues, undeniably important as they were: surgery was a major concern, but I was not performing it; and approval of my role was given tacitly by the very fact that I was hired by the Golden family earlier that day. Above all, our first encounter was an act of confirmation. As I prepared to return home, Margie took me in her arms, and, as she clutched me in a tight embrace, I felt an incredible heat transfer between us. Whether it was from me to her or from her to me, I'm not sure. Nevertheless, we both commented on it. We had known each other personally for only a few hours, and by name for not much longer, but I believe that it was at that moment that a sense of validation descended upon the two of us. She needed to be reassured that she was making the right choice, and in hindsight, perhaps I did as well. It is never easy to allow a virtual stranger to delve into the most intimate corners of your life, and being that virtual stranger is a role not to be taken lightly either. Still, I drove home that night feeling confident; I knew that Margie and I would make a perfect match.

From the moment we met in January until her death nine months later in October, Margie relied on me to be her health advocate, as she grappled with and eventually succumbed to pancreatic cancer, an almost-always fatal form of the insidious disease. However, my advocacy work was nothing more than an extension of her will; no one was a greater advocate for Margie than Margie herself. I was, as Margie often said, "her voice," a close confidante who could remain steadfast in spite of peripheral challenges and distractions. From my intimate viewpoint, I was granted an uninterrupted look at a woman who redefined the meaning of living with strength, and dying with dignity. Comforted by her family and by her beliefs, this amazing lady set off toward a great light, rather than a great darkness, discovering the grace and elegance contained in every waking hour. Watching Margie as she travelled toward death was as edifying as it was painful. To witness the beauty of Margie's death was an honour and a gift—a gift that needs to be communicated.

But I am not the only one who has felt this story was worth sharing. In fact, this book was Margie's idea. She knew that she wasn't going to live forever, but she wanted others to benefit from the lessons that we both learned along the way. And such lessons! I approach each patient today mindful of what I learned during my nine months with Margie, and I strive to approach my own life's journey with the determination and vigour that Margie brought to hers.

> *I want to fully recover from surgery in a calm, pain-managed way, surrounded by kind, sincere people who are gentle, soft-spoken, reassuring, positive and encouraging.*

Margie's stated this unambiguous goal the first time we spoke that January evening. She knew what she wanted, and she trusted me to make it happen for her. It's not easy

4

for anyone entering a completely new and frightening phase of life to articulate an objective as clearly as Margie did. Even more remarkably, Margie had not handled illness, stress and change well in the past. Earlier that day, she had returned by air ambulance to Toronto from Houston, Texas, accompanied by her husband, Saul, some family members, and a doctor. While consulting with cancer specialists at the renowned MD Anderson clinic, Margie was suddenly overcome by the gravity of her situation, and collapsed in fear. She plummeted into a darkness that she had never before experienced. She was hospitalized, and after much thought and family discussion, she decided to return to Toronto to proceed with a recommended surgery. She wanted to be with her whole family and her dear friends, and realized she had to go home. Her daughter-in-law, Jill, had contacted me, and I envisioned managing the care of a woman who, I was told, was dangerously weak, exhausted, and shattered by this unexpected nightmare.

But while we all prepared for the worst, something in Margie changed. For the first time in her life, in the very depths of her darkness, she found a light. As she lay in a Houston hospital, this woman who, at other times, had struggled with the spectre of illness and emotional pain, reached an uncanny ease with her situation and with herself. She had entered the aircraft bed-ridden, but upon landing in Toronto, she exited the plane on her own two feet. Clearly, she had pulled herself out of darkness by making a transformation, so that in her mind she was not a victim, or even a mere passer-by. She had become the leading lady in the drama of her own life, and so she returned to her home and her family with a concrete goal, and a new-found belief in the power of the universe to provide the courage she would need. Out of her doubt, faith emerged, and her new mantra became *God Will Provide.* The new Margie was once again ready to take part in the world she knew.

Before my first visit to the Golden home, I gathered a team of nurses and caregivers to help me guide this lady along the road that lay ahead. Based on what I'd heard from Jill about Margie's catastrophic breakdown in Texas, I was expecting to meet an invalid, a shadow of a woman suffo-cating beneath the combined forces of physical torment and emotional despondency. Instead, I found the exact opposite: a woman rich in natural beauty, with a hard, athletic body and a brilliant head of strikingly silver hair tied back in a ponytail. She wore little make-up – just a pale pink lipstick. She was vibrant and vital, earthy and real. She wanted to talk about her surgery, her recovery, and her future, rather than wallow in endless self-pity.

So I got her to articulate her goals to me, and she frankly confided the belief that led her out of her darkest hours: that God would grant her the strength she needed. Of course she was not immune to fear; no one is. But I was to be her safeguard against excessive fear. Margie understood her limitations and her tendencies, and she realized that any uncertainty with which she couldn't cope might send her back into deep mental anguish. So I had to grant that certainty to her. She needed to know that there was one person who could remain attached and detached simultaneously, who could advocate tirelessly on her behalf without the emotional reactions of a son, a daughter, or a husband. She needed to know that there was someone who could facilitate the gentleness and kindness for which she prayed to be surrounded. My job was to be that facilitator.

About eight months after Margie's death, I spoke with Saul on the telephone. We talk as friends quite often now, the closeness that we achieved during Margie's nine-month long odyssey seemingly stronger in the wake of her passing. This time, he shared with me a conversation that he had with his wife just after our first meeting.

"I asked Marjorie at the very beginning if there was anything that I could do for her," he told me. "She asked only that I allow her to have complete, uninterrupted access to you whenever she wanted."

Those words overwhelmed me. Imagine being so comfortable in your decision that you are willing to put such stock in a stranger! Even before we truly embarked, Margie knew where we were headed: I was to be her voice when she could not speak for herself.

TWO

"She speaks for me."

Margie must have begun to feel like a broken record repeating those words, as my role was put into question from the very first discussions in preparation for her operation, the Whipple procedure. The gallbladder, bile duct, duodenum and the head of the pancreas were coming out; the plumbing was going to be completely reworked. Needless to say, a grand array of doctors, nurses, and lab technicians were involved — and all had trouble understanding exactly what I was doing there alongside Margie and Saul, and why I was the one doing most of the talking. To many of them, I was either a "nosy outsider" or a "meddling insider," and both Margie and I were constantly forced to justify our approach. In truth, our partnership permitted Margie to be the *body* and me to be the *will* whenever we went in for consultations or blood work; before and after, we made sure we were of one mind. There had to be absolute cohesion between what I was saying and what she was feeling.

At the same time, I was just beginning to get to know the Goldens. And, while I always needed to check with Margie to make sure we were on the same page, I knew that nothing should unreasonably infringe upon the tranquility and gentleness that she expected to enjoy throughout the process. At the hospital, on that first day of pre-op, I made a point of putting her written goal into her file and ensuring that the medical staff who would be caring for her were familiar with it. I let everybody know that this lady was going in for surgery within a few days, and found interesting the many looks of surprise that came my way when I made the simple plea to look at Margie as a complete person – a physical and spiritual being. I could not let her lose the sense of control that she tried to keep over her situation; her former despondency and mental paralysis were not far behind her, and I was determined to guard against their return.

When you go into a store to buy a pair of shoes, you

expect the staff to welcome you, act courteously, and generally make sure that you feel good about the experience. Why
should anyone expect anything less when receiving medical
treatment? Twenty-five years ago, when I began working as
a registered nurse, the pre-op interview was in many ways
the most important part of the procedure. The list of questions that nurses had to pose to their patients provided the
opportunity to reassure them about any doubts they might
be having, and to give all of the information regarding the
"before," "during," and "after" phases of the operation. But
twenty-five years later, it's a totally different patient experience. When Margie, Saul and I were interviewed by the
pre-op nurse, she conducted the proceedings with her eyes
fixated on the keys of her computer, expressionlessly typing
the entire time. Margie tried to initiate a conversation,
beginning with a "hello, pleased to meet you", and telling
the nurse that this was all a new experience for her. The
nurse flatly informed her that she was in a hurry, which
put an end to any attempts to open a more personalized
dialogue. Instead, the air was filled with rote questions,
rote answers, and always, endless typing. Eye contact was

non-existent. For me, this incident was a disturbing indication of the new face of public medical service. For Margie, it was a challenge — an opportunity to practice her new commitment to staying positive, to think about the absurdity of it all, and to maintain that tranquil and collected space in which she so desperately wanted to remain.

Despite the unnerving dedication to speed that much of the staff purported to hold, that pre-op day seemed to drag on and on. We spent no less than five hours at the hospital, shuttling ourselves from admissions, to blood tests, to the anaesthetist, to the nurse clinicians. For most people, it would be a day when stress levels would climb through the roof — a five-hour-long stream of discussions about pancreatic cancer would shake anyone. Margie, however, remained relaxed and calm. Already she was able to look at the big picture. It was not about who was inattentive, who was hurried, who was dismissive, or who was condescending; it was about her, and with that she was at peace. She was practising a selective obliviousness, weeding out the negative and holding on to the positive. She was well-trained in tai chi, and so she practised it as she waited, both to pass the time and to calm the nerves. By the end of the day, we were all physically tired and emotionally drained. Nevertheless, Margie's poise throughout the entire process of "hurry-up-and-wait" was remarkable. I was certainly impressed, but I believe she herself was more impressed than anyone. She had recognized that she could be strong and composed and that she could now rest comfortably, knowing that I would make certain she was not overlooked. That first day was a test for both of us, and we passed.

THREE

The days immediately preceding Margie's surgery were, in retrospect, the period when she set the stage for all that was to come. It was then that she established with her family how her care was to be managed; it was then that she established with me exactly how she needed me to pursue those goals for her. As was becoming increasingly evident, Margie approached each turn in the road with perfect clarity. Her wishes were straightforward: only immediate family members were to visit her in the hospital and visits were to be staggered so that she could rest properly. She even put a message on her answering machine that simply said *I am going in for surgery*, and directed callers to telephone her children for more information. She didn't want Saul to be beleaguered by messages at home. The information to her children, in turn, was to be transmitted through me, and I made sure to record each request in writing. Margie needed the security and comfort that only adherence to her wishes could provide.

Despite my growing closeness to Margie, I was very conscious of the fact that I was *not* family. I recognized that I had to tread on delicate ground with Saul. I could not let him feel cast aside, as though I had assumed a very important role in his wife's care at his expense. Furthermore, Saul was no youngster — he was ten years older than his wife. His fear was very real indeed, and seeing his wife struggle with a potentially fatal disease could be overwhelming. My challenge was to subtly demonstrate to Saul that, despite the deep and immediate bond of trust that Margie and I established, I could not be his surrogate, and he need not feel threatened by me. Margie knew that he had a role in her journey, but we needed to allay his fears about the travelling company, if not the journey itself.

Into the whirlwind of action that encompassed the few days before Margie's operation entered another player. Sandra Kohn was Margie and Saul's daughter, who, along with her husband and their three sons, lived full-time in the Rocky Mountain resort town of Park City, Utah.

Sandy immediately made clear that she was in Toronto to stay with her mother for the long haul, and that she expected to participate in a significant way. Of course, she, too, was a little wary about a strange woman running the show, and her decision to move into her parents' home kept her at very close proximity to me. I understood that while the relationship between Margie and me was natural, my relationship with the rest of the family would take some work. The surprise that Sandy might have felt over my presence, and even over Margie's recently-discovered spiritual awareness, however, could not be allowed to derail what Margie and I were trying to accomplish. There was definitely room for Sandy within the support structure that I was building for Margie, though. I decided that a good role for her to fill was as a liaison between me and the family. After all, she would be staying at the house, along with my care staff, and she would be able to transmit any questions that the family, Saul, and Margie had for me whenever they arose. She also could demonstrate confidence to any relatives who were still unsure about me, my approach, and the trust that Margie had in it.

Despite the slight, yet detectable level of tension that existed between me and friends and relatives caught off guard by Margie's sudden ordeal, Margie's commitment to our plan never wavered. We were going forward, always looking ahead, and even though her future was somewhat murky, she refused to let her moment-by-moment life goals fall by the wayside. She would not tolerate pain; her terrible ordeal had to unfold as gently as possible. We devised a pain intensity rating scale from 1 to 10, so that the hospital staff and I could easily identify what to do to assist her. That's the way it was with Margie: she wanted to be on top of everything. The next few days would obviously be a major challenge for her, weakened as she would be by the strains of surgery, but she was determined to remain calm and steady. She courageously refused to lose the control that she retained over herself — it was a source of dignity and pride.

Amongst my most treasured memories of my time with Margie are the telephone messages that she left for me on my machine. I've kept those tapes; to hear her voice again is at once heart-warming and eerie. What stands out, however, is just how strikingly vital that voice sounds. It's not the voice of a dying woman, or a woman labouring under the strain of a fatal disease. It's the sound of a woman who has her act together, who knows where she's going and has trust in how she's getting there. It's a voice that's full of questions, always planning, always looking two steps ahead.

You might say that Margie had the foresight to know that she would soon not have foresight. She prepared for pain before it came; her recovery was planned before surgery began. She was not going to let herself get caught off guard, and she knew that I would be there to keep her on the track that she herself had set. In her own remarkable way, Margie looked to the future, leaving as little as possible to chance.

The night before Margie's operation, I couldn't settle to sleep easily. I was thinking about the coming day, and when I picked up Margie, Saul, and Sandra in the morning to take them to the hospital, I could tell that they, too, had experienced restless nights. Nevertheless, despite the collective case of nerves, a palpable air of optimism pervaded the car. Following that night of tossing and turning, it was oddly refreshing to see Margie once again stridently upbeat, resolved not to let the obvious fear drag her down. She wanted to take this attitude all the way to the operating room.

"Andrea," she said, "I don't want them to sedate me before they give me the anaesthetic. I really don't want to be out of it." As always, Margie wanted complete clarity throughout as much of the procedure as possible. She knew that her illness had her down; she was determined to prove that she was not out.

Nevertheless, visions of the collapse in Texas flashed through my mind. Although the Margie that I knew was seemingly a pillar of strength, I had my doubts as to whether, left to her own devices, Margie could fend off a recurrence of her past malaise alone. I decided to ask the nursing staff whether I would be permitted to accompany Margie all the way to the operating room. I suggested that I would be able to help steady her nerves, thereby making the job easier for the doctors and nurses involved. Like many of my other appeals, consent was given in stages. At first, they thought we were crazy. Then, they *knew* we were crazy: they watched as Margie passed the time spent in pre-op with yoga, tai chi, and meditative breathing exercises. Obviously, this was a scene that not many nurses had viewed before.

Margie, for her part, was becoming a little self-conscious. "Is this okay?" she asked me, quizzically looking around the room and meeting many pairs of staring eyes.

I did my best to reassure her. "You do whatever you need," I told her. "This is your surgery". She had to do what was right for herself, and if entering the operating room in a positive frame of mind meant practising East Asian relaxation techniques in the pre-op waiting lounge, so be it. This surgery didn't belong to the doctors, the nurses, the hospital, or even to me; it was about Margie. Her body, her strength, and her health belonged to her.

Although our behaviour in the hospital was some-what alternative, it was evident that we knew what we were doing — after all, yoga in the hospital isn't something done spontaneously or without thinking. Fortunately, I was permitted to follow Margie until we reached the door of the operating room. She stayed calm, and I stayed on top of her particular situation, reminding the nurses of Margie's allergies to various morphines, penicillin, and sulphas. I found that even though her allergies were listed clearly in her file, in many cases that information had not been relayed. Of course, I took care of this issue without bothering Margie; it was not her job — it was mine. I allowed Margie to leave the worrying to me — she had a major challenge ahead of her, and that was more than enough to handle.

When I left Margie, she was entering the operating room just as she had wished: calm, confident, alert, yet fully at peace. Back in the waiting room, I found Saul and Sandy, along with Jill and her husband, Michael, and Margie's youngest son, Terry and his wife, Cindy, all anxiously sitting in wait. A heightened level of stress ran through everyone, especially Saul. I told him about the cool disposition that his wife took into surgery, and I assured all of them that I would remain at the hospital and keep them informed of what transpired. Still, they stayed. They stayed because they wanted to be there as Margie went through her ordeal, really just to be close to her. Some went out for

a breath of fresh air, but soon returned. Throughout it all,

I waited with them at the hospital. I was given information

on how the operation was progressing from the nursing

staff, and, I immediately reported any news I received to

the family — both those holding vigil and the extended

family — so that no one had to face the greatest of fears,

the fear of the unknown.

Although the tension was thick and heavy around

us, we strove for an upbeat outlook, just as Margie herself

did. Adrenaline was pumping through all of us: when we'd

receive a good report from the operating room, we'd get

into a tight circle and hold hands, and someone might cry

or scream. Emotions were on display for all to see and we

shared the intensity of those moments completely. Nine

hours after our vigil began, the surgery was complete.

FOUR

We met Margie in the recovery room. Her surgery had been a success, and she retained that serenity that she had displayed prior to entering the operating room. Though resting, she remained sharp, decisive, and keen. Margie refused to believe that her large scar should be a source of shame. She chose instead to celebrate any possibility that could extend her life and in fact, called it her "lifeline". She didn't mind letting everyone see it.

While Saul and his children spent their time with Margie, I decided to introduce myself and my role to the post-op staff on hand. Margie had already informed them that someone from outside of her family had been delegated to assume responsibility for addressing her problems and concerns. Nevertheless, my self-introduction was met with a fair amount of stonewalling. The staff had such difficulty comprehending that this patient had actually hired someone to advocate on her behalf that their first response was to resist the concept itself. I realized that if I couldn't convince them to agree with me, I had to at least get them to tolerate me. To that extent, it would be a bit of an educational process for everybody — doctors, nurses, and me.

I decided to identify myself to the unit manager. I explained that the family had hired Qualicare to work for them, and for me to speak on their behalf. I informed her of my plans to provide personal caregivers for the patient both at the hospital and at home, and let her know that I would be present at all meetings with the doctors and at all discussions over Margie's hospital discharge and aftercare. Once again, I was surprised by the ambivalent reaction that I received. She actually took it rather personally, as though I was trying to tell her how to do her job. I explained that I was not trying to be her temporary supervisor; I was only speaking for Margie — asking the right questions, getting the tough answers, working through the difficult decisions. Moreover, I stressed that her personal opinion notwithstanding, it was Margie's opinion that mattered most: I would be involved as long as she wanted me to work on her behalf. There was nothing at all illegitimate about what Margie and I were doing. Once she finally understood that there was no real choice in the matter, the unit manager actually became rather agreeable. In fact, her reaction became a common pattern I noticed: initial distrust, reluctance, and finally, acceptance and eventual appreciation of the value of the service to both the patient and the system. It's hard to argue with a fait accompli.

Admittedly, the very nature of my role and of my company appears to challenge the status quo. Many people in the healthcare field aren't used to being viewed as spokes in the wheel that comprises a patient's care program. They are unaccustomed to dealing with an assertive patient or patient's representative, and subsequently feel affronted by it. For my part, I'm saddened to see a doctor or nurse dismiss the value of this worthwhile service. As long as one doctor is not assigned just one patient, it makes perfect sense to have another qualified person involved who can manage the assortment of care and treatment options with which a patient is faced. We all accept that if you want to build a house, you call a general contractor; if you want to

decorate it, you call a designer. We accept that there are
experts who can play an integral role in evaluating the
various options and tailoring them to their clients' needs. We
mustn't lower our expectations when it comes to our health.

My biggest supporter, as always, was Margie.
During her seven-day recovery stay at the hospital, we held
daily meetings to review her goals and discharge wishes.
Whenever she'd encounter resistance to her plans and ideas
from staff, I reminded her to keep her sights trained forward. It was tough for her, though. She knew that we had
to be polite, non-threatening and generally pleasant, but
she couldn't get over the dismissive, even rude, attitude
that some who were supposed to be aiding her displayed.
Moreover, when I wasn't there, she felt as though she had
to deal with the conflicts by herself, and that was exactly
what she wanted *not* to do.

"Everything we're doing is legit," I said. "If they
don't want to listen to you, just tell them it's been okayed
by the unit manager."

I made sure that I immediately met with the staff
on hand and informed them that questions about Margie's

care were to be put through me at her request. But, at heart, I found the flippant attitude of many people toward Margie's requests to be extremely unfair. We weren't asking everybody to agree with us; we only asked that they acknowledge that there are different ways of doing things, and the health advocacy option was the one Margie chose. This route, after all, was hers to choose.

"Rest" was the operative word once Margie came home from the hospital. She had a feeling that she'd be the type of person who would want to push herself physically to do perhaps more than she should, and she wanted us to be aware of it in advance. I say "us", because by this stage I had a whole team involved. I coordinated a group of personal support workers to accompany Margie around the clock, and I organized frequent visits from a masseuse in order to aid in the relaxation and recovery regime. I instructed them all to encourage Margie to rest; she wanted to get her strength back as quickly as possible. Margie also had to get used to her new body. We had a consultation with a dietician, in order to become a little more educated about how her eating would be different: Margie had a great deal of "new plumbing" inside of her to get used to. She had me take notes during the consultation, so that if she had any questions later, I could explain what she either didn't understand or needed to have repeated.

Margie was particularly interested in the new-fangled inner workings of her body. She had always been proud of her scar, but now she wanted to take a look at what exactly had been done to her. I printed off pictures of the Whipple procedure that I found on the Internet, and Margie often asked me to review them with her. It made the whole experience a little more real for her. Neither dwelling on the surgery nor looking at the scar gave her any discomfort. In fact, for Margie both were emblematic of how fortunate she was. The tumour that had been removed was not yet that large, and she was thankful that it was caught early. Her hope was that she might still be able to be fully cured and live. The real times of trouble came in the evening. Then, all of the emotions that churned within her behind that brave public face rose to the surface. There were tears — a lot of tears — and questions and prayers. She was worried — how could anyone not be? What if the surgery wasn't successful? What if the cancer had spread? She knew that it was out of her hands, but to reconcile herself to this possibility wasn't easy for her. I visited her on some of those nights. I reminded her that the only thing that she could control was healing — taking care of herself after the operation. Despite the intense fears, she had to persevere, and fight through them. If she didn't take proper care of herself, going forward might be even more difficult; she had to be both physically repaired and emotionally prepared to face possible future challenges. So she'd struggle through it, and in the end, she'd find the positives: she was still alive, she was getting better, and she had complete family support through it all. Finally she would come back to her mantra, *God Will Provide.* As long as she was doing all she could to heal, she wasn't letting anybody down.

FIVE

Needless to say, I didn't spend all of my time at the Goldens' house. I had my own family to tend to, as well as a number of other clients for whom I was either directly or indirectly responsible. During these early stages of getting Margie settled back at home, I tried to stop by at least once a day for a couple of hours, to make sure everything was on track, and that Margie was comfortable with the progress she was making. Much of the day-to-day work was done by a team of personal caregivers. I ensured that the ladies I chose were supportive, nurturing, calm, and encouraging, in order to meet the goals Margie had set for herself. Each one was different, and each developed a unique relationship with Margie — she even sang with some of them! The level of closeness between Margie and her numerous caregivers obviously varied; nevertheless, she let each one of them know just how valuable they were to her, and to the success of her journey.

Even though I put the pieces of the care puzzle together, it was Margie who really set the mood — always positive, and always comforting.

The biggest challenge faced by the caregivers, and by myself, was keeping Margie in bed. She wanted to be up and active, looking after her house, cooking, cleaning. She wanted to feel normal again. But whenever she'd try to run the show, she'd end up exhausted; she just couldn't do it yet. I had to be straight with her.

"Margie, you can't keep getting out of bed whenever you see something that needs attention. Where you're needed is here. You must build up your reserves," I insisted, pointing to her bed.

"I feel so useless lying down all the time," she argued. "It's just so hard."

"The more rest you get, the sooner you'll be able to get back into your old routine. You've got to save as much energy as you can. Right now your job is to get better."

That didn't sit very well with her. She knew I was right, and she listened to me, but that didn't make it any easier.

Unfortunately, the end of Margie's surgery did not signal the end of Margie's invasive treatments: in order to increase her odds of defeating this cancer, she had to look now toward chemotherapy. As soon as she began to feel strong enough, she was scheduled for eight chemo sessions at the hospital. Margie fully understood that this leg of the journey would not be gentle. Still, it was a concession she was willing to make in the name of a full recovery.

We checked in at the front desk of the day treatment chemotherapy department for Margie's first session, and then took our seats in the waiting room. Beside the doorway leading to the treatment room stood a giant gong. I asked a passing nurse what it was doing there.

"Oh, you must be new here," she said. "Whenever a patient finishes his last chemo session, he gets to ring the gong – you know, kind of to celebrate."

As soon as the nurse had walked on, Margie turned to me, a look of incredulity on her face.

"That's ridiculous!" she said. "This is my first session — I've got seven more to go. What if I don't make it? Do I *never* get to ring the gong?"

"You know what, Margie?" I replied. "You can ring the gong whenever you want."

"You mean it?" she asked.

I could tell that this was about more than the shrill peal of the gong. Such a small-minded rule seemed absurd.

"Why not? There's no reason patients shouldn't be able to celebrate an accomplishment. You're about to have your first treatment, and that's an accomplishment in itself. If you feel positive and want to ring the gong afterwards, go ahead."

A few hours later, Margie and I exited the treatment area through the door to the waiting room. She lifted the mallet and struck the gong firmly in the center. A loud chime rang out through the room, followed immediately by a shower of applause. Clapping hands greeted Margie as she and I walked through the room.

"I did it!" she said to me in a loud but conspiratorial whisper.

We held hands and headed for the main door. As we exited, I turned and beheld the enormous smile that wreathed Margie's face.

That day, Margie redefined the terms of success, or at least, the measure of victory. Defeating her disease once and for all would be the big victory, but every morning that she woke up ready to tackle the challenges of the day was a victory in itself. Completing eight sessions of chemotherapy would be good, but getting through even one wasn't bad either.

In the end, Margie made it through five chemotherapy sessions. During all of those visits to the hospital, we never once heard anybody else ring the gong; it sat silently idle by the door, waiting for someone — anyone — to successfully run the chemo gauntlet. Margie had wisely decided not to wait until it was too late to celebrate something that might never happen. Whenever she had the chance to celebrate, she took it.

SPRING

SIX

Margie was a vigorous, healthy woman: her scar healed quickly, and she easily slipped back into her routine. She was proud of the recovery that she had made, and although she still had to battle through rounds of chemotherapy, she believed that she was making progress. Saul, too, seemed relieved — the initial shock had subsided, and he had regained that spark in his life that Margie's illness and subsequent risky surgery had all but extinguished. Sandra went back home to Utah to be with her family, and to decompress. My visits to the Golden home became less frequent. Though we still talked every day, daily visits were no longer necessary. In short, we were all getting back to normal, or as normal as possible.

It was May 8th that Margie began to feel that something was just not right. After consulting with her surgeon, she was booked for a CT scan on May 15th, so that we could find out what was going on. Margie was frustrated by what she believed was the inability of any doctor to pinpoint exactly what was wrong with her, and she also became concerned that her worrying was burning me out. She began to need much more face-to-face, emotional support from me, and I sought to calm her, so that she could approach the situation with the clarity that she desired. Waiting for that test proved difficult for us. I believe that we both secretly knew what the problem had to be — the cancer must have spread — but we could not allow ourselves to think that way. We had to look at the upcoming CT scan as a source of information, rather than of despair.

The scan found an abnormality in the liver, which the doctor said could mean one of two things. First, it could be some sort of abscess. This, he told us, was unlikely. There were no signs that Margie had developed some new infection. The only other possibility was the one that we feared the most, yet also expected: the cancer had metastasized. The doctor suggested that Margie have an abdominal ultrasound. She was booked for May 26th.

The ten days between the two appointments served to delay the inevitable. We hadn't yet discussed how we would proceed with treatment, but we knew that the journey would soon reach a critical juncture. The emotional strain was taking its toll on Margie, and she felt a need to get away from it all: away from hospitals, away from Toronto, and away from a mindset that looked ahead and only saw death. The next day she called to tell me that she and Saul were going up north to their cottage on Lake Muskoka. I agreed it would be good for her to relax, see some friends, and get outdoors. She needed to do some living. Margie ended the call with a plea that gripped me with the power of her words, and the intensity of her voice.

"Don't you give up on me," she said. "Andrea, don't give up."

SEVEN

A major change came over Margie while she was up at the cottage. Finally, she was able to distance herself from the antiseptic world of hospitals and surgical gloves, and immerse herself in the boundless expanses of nature. She swam and hit golf balls at the driving range; she saw friends and entertained for them. Every experience became another opportunity to see the beauty in the everyday — sunset over the lake, the gentle laugh of a friend, or quiet time spent alone with Saul on the dock. She knew that she would probably be coming home to bad news; nevertheless, she was fully focussed on enjoying life and its often-overlooked pleasures. Despite the knowledge that she was weakening physically, she couldn't help but feel happy. In the company of her family, close friends and Saul, she felt so protected and supported. She fed off the energy that those closest to her brought to her life.

"Andrea," she told me over the telephone, "when I get away from the city I have so much time to think, and I realize how totally blessed I am to have Saul, and my wonderful family, and my friends. When I step back from the stress and the frustration, all I can see is how lucky I am."

That was her moment of self-validation. Our embrace at the end of our first meeting had validated my role in her journey, and that visit to the cottage substantiated the truth of her core belief.

Margie returned to Toronto on May 25th. The city, she was discovering now, was toxic to her. When she returned, she realized how much better she felt up north. At the lake there was peace, beauty, and tranquility, while the city for her began to represent stress, insecurity, and death. She needed to be in tune with nature, in tune with herself.

The ultrasound on May 26th proved what we feared, but also expected. The cancer had metastasized to the liver, and new tumours were visible on the ultrasound. The doctor authorized my request to refer Margie to the

Temmy Latner Center for Palliative Care, a Toronto-based, multidisciplinary palliative care service. I had worked with this organization on numerous occasions in the past, and had always been impressed with the high level of care, respect, and dignity they gave to my clients and their families. We had scheduled a meeting with the oncologist to discuss any further options, but as Margie had already gone through surgery and then chemotherapy, we knew that options would be few and far between. Any steps would only serve to delay the inevitable! She knew that she was going to die.

Back home again, she informed Saul; I telephoned Sandy in Park City, to explain what the ultrasound had found. In turn, she relayed the message to the rest of her family, telling them as much as we knew up until then. On that day, every one of us faced the reality of Margie's imminent death. But Margie's attitude was that she had been blessed in life; she now had to go out and seize whatever was left of it. She was not going to fade away into the sunset – she was going to flourish during the days left to her.

Margie no longer really spoke about beating the odds; she understood what was in store for her. And yet, although she was resigned to her fate, she was not resigned to giving up. Margie wanted the world to share the zest with which she cherished her life, and it was then that she decided that we should tell her story and write this book, not as a lamentation, but as a celebration.

EIGHT

In my work as a nurse, I often found myself drawn into situations with terminally ill patients, and they often chose their last moments with me by their side. I didn't mind this type of work and I carried on supporting people as they died. Nevertheless, I began to notice a pattern among these patients as their lives wound down. A delicate calm would overcome them, complete with an acceptance of what was to happen, and faith in what was to come. It was as though they were receiving some sort of message: that everything would be okay; that they could relax; that the journey would be gentle. I could never really comprehend where exactly this message was coming from; I just knew that my duty was to allow my patients to reach this peaceful state, and let them enjoy these moments in which they seemingly wandered between the material and the empyreal. Even so, I knew that something greater than my efforts alone must have been at work within my

patients. A moment of extreme alertness would overwhelm

them, not long before their passing. They would tell me of a

beautiful place that they knew they were approaching, and

the descriptions were so vivid that the image of it seemed

to be right before their eyes. Time and time again I would

hear these descriptions, always uttered in a moment of

complete — almost omniscient — clarity. This ever-growing

mystery, and my inability to explain it, mystified me. I had

to figure this thing out.

I began to explore the nature of spirituality, and

what it adds to our lives. The more I explored, the more all

things made sense to me — I began to understand just how

my dying patients could become so trusting and so peaceful

as the end was approaching.

When my husband and I finally decided to build

Qualicare, we did so with an incredible resource behind us:

truth. Working with my clients during their more difficult

moments, I found myself increasingly comfortable with the

concept of sharing thoughts, fears and hopes with them. And

once we had achieved that level of connectedness, we became

much more unified in purpose, and certain in our actions.

I know that my comfort with spirituality made me more valuable to Margie. She was a deeply spiritual person, and knew that those around her were not; they turned away from the metaphysical while she embraced it. She needed to feed off of what I had embraced, and by doing so she was able to help others to appreciate the spiritual nature at the heart of her final grand adventure. She wanted others to see what she saw, to feel the way she felt; and she wanted me to guide her along the way. That was the beauty of my relationship with Margie: it was so pure, and so spiritual — it was complete care, and we both knew it. And all the while, she kept giving — to her friends, to her family, to Saul, and to me. She took, too, but that's what you do in a relationship; you have to take to give.

The morning after the meeting in which we finally were forced to confront the inevitability of Margie's death, Margie emerged from her sleep unfazed.

"I'm getting on with my life," she announced, as she walked out the door and headed to her exercise class. She wasn't going to let anything stop her; she was not going to write death a blank cheque. Margie was determined not to forfeit the end of her life to defeat and despair.

As June began, Margie's eagerness to explore her own future was keeping me rather occupied. I was immersed in exploring all options. We wanted to look at new therapies, new choices, new remedies. Many times Margie herself took the lead: she'd call to tell me about a doctor she had heard of, a new research possibility, or some homeopathic regime. While she was doing her homework, I tried to figure out which treatments were appropriate for pancreatic cancer, and for her circumstances. I had to strike a balance between Margie's desire to experiment with all sorts of alternative treatments and the reality that we would have to make choices — we could not try absolutely everything. Many of the naturopathic remedies that we discovered were exorbitantly expensive, especially in light of the minimal benefits that they promised. Others had a great risk of side effects. I had to keep on top of all of these extra possibilities, while at the same time pursuing traditional medical options.

Ever since the referral to the Temmy Latner Center, I had been exploring the variety of services that they offered in the hopes that I might find something beneficial to our particular situation. The breadth and depth of their services greatly impressed me. Furthermore, I began to work with Dr. Ron Davis, a truly humane and thoughtful palliative care physician, who enthusiastically supported my philosophy and the care structure that I was trying to create. I knew that if I was going to make this a successful experience for Margie and her family, I needed his expertise and the support of the Temmy Latner Center.

The Latner Center emphasized body and mind connection — exactly what I was interested in pursuing with Margie. As recovery was no longer in the cards, we incorporated the Center's offerings into our overarching goal of enriching the life left to be lived — which would incorporate focusing on Margie's core beliefs, decreasing stress levels, ensuring time for relaxation, nurturing the relationships that were most important to her, and maintaining a daily routine that was as normal as possible.

Despite the tremendously brave face Margie put on, early June was not an easy time for her. Now that she knew that the end of her days would not be a matter of "sometime," but of "sometime soon," everything she did was influenced, often subconsciously, by this knowledge. She was committed to staying positive, but thoughts of sadness nevertheless crept into her mind. A meeting with a trusted and longtime family doctor convinced her that she needed to get away for a while. Margie and Saul once again headed up north to their cottage for a few days, to take a break from the pressures at home. As before, Margie returned to join me for a trip to see the oncologist. Although she did her best to relax by the lake and distance herself from the worries that so often accompanied her, reality was never far away.

SUMMER

NINE

I spoke to Margie immediately after she returned from the cottage in early June. She had enjoyed her getaway with Saul out of the city, but now knew that it was nearing the time to make her big decision. How did she want to go forward? Our scheduled meeting with the oncologist would help clarify the choices for her.

There were really only three options: she could continue with the chemotherapy, as she had done for the last few months; she could do nothing, and have another CT scan in a few months; or she could try an experimental trial chemo treatment, that had been made available at the hospital on that very day. We discussed these options with the oncologist, and I obtained a lot of information on the clinical trial, but Margie was still unsure of how she wanted to proceed. She just wanted to return to her cottage, and leave the world of hospitals, painful treatments and stress behind her. She asked me to review the options for her while she was away.

But a few days later, she called to explain that she had decided she wanted to focus on the quality of her life. Although the hours spent in the hospital were potentially increasing the quantity of her days, the pain of chemotherapy was decreasing their quality. While away from the hospitals, she was truly enjoying her life. She was experiencing an incredible amount of kindness and love from friends and family, which crystallized for her sense of gratitude. She had made her choice.

"I can't tolerate any further treatment at this time."

Her voice brimmed with emotion as she spoke those words — not the emotion of sadness or despair, but of empowerment.

"I'm not giving up," she said. "I'm still in charge."

And she was. Hours spent in hospitals, coping with the harsh, burning sensation of chemotherapy, was decreasing her joy. Better to spend time up at the lake, with Saul, with family or with friends. That, she realized, was the ultimate priority.

She wanted to blossom. She knew that, like a flower, this one summer was all she had. After that, she would wither, and then drift away. But now she wanted to unfurl her petals to the world — to take in the beauty of all that she cherished: nature, her relationships, and her growing appreciation of the miracles that define our days. Death was a miracle, she realized, no different than the miracle of birth. *What was alive is now dead; what was nonexistent is now alive.* And the processes were also marvelous: growing, then shrinking; getting stronger, then growing weaker. She was flourishing in this mode of constant discovery.

And although Margie still felt relatively strong, the early summer saw her display a remarkable openness about death. It wasn't fatalistic, or morbid; it was accepting. She wasn't hoping to die. She just knew that for now, she was going to live, and whatever would happen, would happen, regardless of whether she wanted it or not. Saul, Sandy, and I often found ourselves talking about what would take place once Margie was gone, only to realize that Margie was right there, participating in the conversation. The topic was not taboo for her. In fact, she'd bring it up herself. Many times, Margie would just start telling me about what she wanted said about her when she was gone — who would deliver the eulogy, what she'd like them to focus on.

Margie would also confide in me her deep concern for Saul after her death. She was not afraid—their discussion about a future without her felt totally normal at the time. Then, I'd sit back and reflect about just how extraordinary it was that this woman had already achieved such a heightened level of composure about her fate. I was witness to an amazing display of trust and deep faith during the last months of Margie's life. She did not allow the untimely end that awaited her to put a damper on this second wind that blew powerfully through her, and invigorated her days.

But while Margie sought to take full advantage of every moment, she increasingly discovered the inability of others to look past her illness.

"Whenever I'm around, people are always feeling sad," she complained. "I feel like saying, *Don't cry for me! I'm through with feeling sorry for myself.*"

"What do they do?" I asked.

"Oh, they're always talking about my disease with

me, like I have nothing else to talk about. And they look so glum all the time! I'm still alive. I can still talk about things besides cancer!"

Some people's reactions unfortunately produced an unnecessarily negative vibe, and limited the number of circles in which Margie felt comfortable. She was a seasoned world traveler accustomed to a significant degree of social prominence, and this need for adjustment in her societal spheres at the same time as so many other adjustments weighed upon her as an unwelcome burden. The only time she truly felt comfortable was when she was alone with Saul. She'd tell me about how wonderful their time up at the cottage was, and just how at peace she felt when the two of them were together. For Saul, the shock of her sickness stung the fiercest, yet he saw how willingly she embraced this newfound opportunity to thrive. Self-pity would have to wait; this shooting star was passing before his eyes, and he did not want to miss a moment of its trajectory.

Anger was certainly not absent from Margie's days. She had come to terms with how her lot had been cast, but she did not wish for death, and the disappointment that she felt was real. Moreover, as she became more and more in touch with her needs, she began to realize how many of them were no longer being properly satisfied. She knew that I was not giving up on her. Even so, she constantly reminded me *never* to give up on her. That was her most important need: to know that she and I were on the same page at all times.

Beyond that, Margie and I began to take an even more assertive role in assembling her care team. She had decided to look for another oncologist. It was not that the one she had was unsatisfactory, only that he really didn't seem to buy in to her approach. In her mind, it was counterproductive to her goals for her remaining days to have in such a critical role someone who was not fully comfortable with her expressed wishes. Fortunately, we were able to find another oncologist with whom we could explore options. Margie let him know her ground rules — *If you find anything that could save my life, go ahead and do it;*

if not, gentleness and quality of life trump all else — and
he accepted them.

The pieces of the puzzle were slowly, but surely,
coming together.

Sandra had returned to Toronto around the middle
of June. She'd planned to stay for the rest of the month,
but she didn't really go home very much after that. I had
to put her to work fairly quickly as family liaison: Margie
was constantly asking me to update *everybody* in her family
about how everything was going, and wanted to make sure
that we were all in sync with one another. She had gone
through her "acceptance phase", but now she had moved on
and was remarkably vigorous.

A visit to a naturopath unexpectedly provided a
major turning point for Margie. In the middle of an appointment, she had lapsed into a "why me?" tirade, and became
rather difficult. But rather than trying to quell her anger,
the naturopath upbraided her. He told her bluntly that
she was throwing a tantrum, and that she was wasting an

incredible amount of energy by getting all worked up about something that she could not control.

"What you can control," he told her, "is your attitude. That's where you can make the biggest difference."

She really seemed to take those words to heart. In a sense, they began to liberate her from her own body. It was her attitude and her outlook that were important. Her success, however it was defined, depended on her mental state. She was not going to restrain her mind any longer: she was going to speak up for herself even more clearly, and I knew that she expected me to do so as well.

Although Margie spent much of early July up at the cottage, I kept close tabs on her, and it was comforting to hear how well she was doing.

"You know what, Andrea? I'm really feeling pretty normal now." She was playing golf — not just hitting balls — but making it through eighteen holes. She was sleeping well, her appetite was good and, amazingly, her weight was increasing.

On July 15th, back in the city, I accompanied Margie to her CT scan. We returned to the hospital the next day to meet with the new oncologist and discuss what the scan had revealed. Unfortunately, the computer systems were down and the doctor was unable to get the results of the scan, but he told us that, no matter what the tests showed, there were really only two options: either she could try chemotherapy again or she could do nothing and just let nature take its course. Needing some time to think about the choice that faced her, Margie went back up north.

For a few days, no one could get in touch with her. She still called me occasionally, but she wasn't really returning anybody else's calls. She told me that she was enjoying spending her time with Saul — trying to recapture the sense of normalcy that she had felt during her last visit. Our conversations were not long; she was always moving — golf, swimming, you name it – and then falling into bed at night, exhausted. She was really trying to get as much out of life as she could. Margie celebrated her birthday on the 26th, and she did so with Saul. On the 30th, she was once again back in the city with me, and heading once more to see the oncologist.

This time, the doctor had the test results ready. The scan showed an increase of metastases to the liver. This was not a surprise, but it opened the door to repeat the question: *what did Margie want to do?*

Margie's decision was aided by at least two factors. The new doctor was affiliated with a different cancer care institution. By all accounts, it was a very pleasant chemotherapy day treatment center. And second, the last few weeks had been so full of joy for Margie that her resolve to live and to look positively toward life was strengthened. Although she did not want to interfere with the felicity of her days, she decided to begin chemotherapy again.

She was not without reservations, however. She was worried about the pain — about the interference with her quality of life — and concerned that she might not be capable of making the proper choices for her future as the treatment progressed. That was when she turned to me, her tone quiet but determined. "Andrea," she said, "remember — don't let me suffer any pain. Don't let anyone prolong my life if I'm uncomfortable."

TEN

The plans to recommence the chemotherapy treatment did not last for long. I got a call from Saul a few days after the appointment. They were up north; Margie had suffered an obstruction, and she was now in hospital in the town of Bracebridge. I cancelled the chemo, and contacted the Bracebridge hospital. Margie had been admitted immediately, and was on IV; the doctors suggested to me that she return to Toronto, to be under the care of her own doctor, and to have another CT scan done on the area. That was when I realized that Margie's desire to remain up north as much as possible would inevitably conflict with her worsening condition. Clearly, we had to prepare for palliative care in the Muskokas, as well. I was determined to leave nothing to chance.

As soon as Margie was able to leave the hospital, not repaired but at least stabilized, she returned along with Sandra and Saul to Toronto. We went to see the surgeon, who validated what we already knew: the obstruction was caused either by adhesions or further metastases. Beyond that, he wasn't sure. As for the CT scan, that would have to wait as well – the surgeon felt that it would be better to have it taken when Margie was in pain; apparently, her pain was not severe enough.

"So why don't you go back up north," he suggested, "and come down if it's bothering you. We can get these tests done then."

And so, when she felt another painful episode coming on, she raced back to the city, to find out what it was, what she should do — to find out *anything*. But all we'd get was hedging and half-committals. We certainly heard a lot about what the doctors *thought* might be causing her pain – but beyond that, no confirmation of any kind. Margie was in and out of the hospital, for more and more tests – in order to confirm a test to confirm another test, and so on. Meanwhile, time was slipping away and Margie was becoming disillusioned with the system. No one could satisfactorily tell her what was happening to her.

Maybe it was difficult for the doctor to talk about

dying. It's hard for a lot of people — a lot of doctors, in
particular. Perhaps knowing the science of it so intimately,
makes the reality hard to face, especially when the reality
comes in the form of a vital and charismatic lady with a
mind as razor-sharp and penetrating as her questions. But
she was comfortable with death — not looking forward to it,
but comfortable with it — and thirsted for the knowledge
that could help her map out the final stages of her life.
And yet, the answers she received were vague, and the
sheer number of tests and scans behind these inconclusive
opinions created doubts in her mind about how much was
really known, and how much she was being told.

As August began, Margie started to feel a different
sort of fatigue, one that she had never experienced before.
She was wearing out — and she knew it. Because she was
not in any sort of extreme pain, she remained up at the cottage. That all changed on the ninth: her excruciating pain
returned, and she headed immediately to the city.

On all levels, the experience at the hospital on that
day was atrocious. Margie couldn't help herself from keeling
over in the lobby, and at one point, collapsed onto the floor.

I quickly righted her, and sat her back up. What startled me, however, was the complete lack of regard paid to us by the hospital staff. An infirm woman was prone on the floor, and the people from the triage team did not even look her way.

I approached the nurses to intercede on Margie's behalf. "Excuse me," I said, forcefully but politely, "this lady I'm with has terminal cancer, and she's feeling very sick."

No eyes met mine.

"Now, she's only here," I continued, "to get a CT scan that the surgeon asked for — otherwise she wouldn't be here right now. But she really needs a bed; I can tell she's going to be sick." No eye contact.

"We don't have any beds. Sorry."

"Well, she can't just vomit in the waiting room here!"

"Here's a kidney basin — she can vomit in that."

And so she did. I was incensed by the incredible indifference upon which my reasonable pleas fell. I brought out all of the records that I kept regarding Margie's condition — that she was a palliative patient; that she had metastatic cancer of the pancreas; that she was here on her doctor's request; and repeated that she urgently needed a place to rest — all in the hope that a paper record could convince the nurses where I could not. Eventually, I was able to secure a bed for Margie. I believe they gave her one just to shut me up.

While the bed was being prepared, Margie turned to me.

"Andrea, I know that you're going to make sure that I stay comfortable, but I just realized that there's one other thing I need you to do."

"What's that?" I asked. Given the time and place of the request, I was sure this was going to be interesting.

Margie's eyes scanned the room. "Please don't let me look horrible. I don't want to look like this: my hair's all messed up, and my mouth isn't clean. If I've got to go, I want to go with my dignity."

"Of course, Margie, I can do that," I assured her.

She never ceases to amaze me, I thought, smiling to myself. No matter her physical condition, her mind was always one step ahead of the game.

I arranged for Margie's facial creams, hair brush,

and toothbrush to be brought to the hospital. Frequent "freshening up" became a part of our routine. Her face was always smooth, soft and radiant. Her hair was always brushed back in a tight pony tail. Her breath was always fresh. It was not about vanity — far from it. Despite her state, Margie wanted to be regarded as a lady, not a liability. Even when she had a tube running out of her nose, I ensured that she smelled nice. She was ill — that was all. She still had her dignity to maintain.

Eventually, Margie was given the CT scan for which we had come in the first place. As expected, it revealed an obstruction where the bowels joined, and again we were back at the original conclusion — it could be adhesions or it could be metastases. The doctors and nurses suggested that a surgical procedure could clear up the obstruction.

"How long would the recovery period be?" I asked.

"Oh, probably two weeks, or so."

Margie recognized that surgery was not an optimal use of her remaining days. She was dying anyway; she wanted to spend her time with her family, not stuck in

the hospital. Ultimately, she decided to allow her body to

recover in the hospital for a short while, before returning

to the lake. I cancelled for good our remaining plans with

the new oncologist. Chemotherapy was now clearly out of

the question — Margie was indisputably a palliative care

patient.

One day after returning to the cottage, Margie

obstructed again, and landed back in Bracebridge Hospital.

I figured that I had to bring the discharge planners at

Bracebridge into the loop: chances were good that Margie

would end up in the hospital again, and perhaps even die

there. I told them our whole story — how Margie wanted

to enhance the quality of her days; how she valued a gentle

death; how she wanted to die at home, surrounded by family

and friends.

My experience with the Bracebridge staff was com-

pletely refreshing. They were so open to helping in any

way they could. They committed themselves wholeheart-

edly to fulfilling Margie's wishes, and they were prepared

to work with me and my care team to ensure that any

transition from Toronto to Bracebridge was seamless. If Margie wanted to be up north, there would be assistance up north; if she wanted to be in the city, we would provide the assistance in the city. Through their willingness to adapt to Margie, rather than insist that the adaptation occur the other way around, the Bracebridge discharge planners reinforced my belief that interest in the patient and their personal care requirements, need not be sacrificed in the world of modern medicine. Their help was unreservedly appreciated.

Time had suddenly accelerated, and was dangerously close to getting out of control. Margie and I had, of course, discussed her death earlier, but now that it was not just a distant abstraction but an impending reality, I knew that we had to refortify our position. I called a big meeting toward to end of August. I asked Margie's palliative care doctor to attend, and I told Sandy to invite the whole family as well. As Margie deteriorated before our eyes, I had to make sure that everyone was on track.

I always tell my clients to feel free to share — to express their emotions during times of physical distress. My approach is all about being open — open to discussion, open to questioning, open to new conclusions. Margie brought a great burden to the table, but by unpacking it to share with me and others, the hurt dissipated. Where most would see despair ahead of them, Marjorie Golden saw hope. She was finally free of her past, and her last months had presented a new lease on life.

When Margie and Saul, their children and spouses, Dr. Davis, and myself were all assembled in the living room of the Golden home, Margie started to speak. She once again reminded her family that she wanted to remain as comfortable as possible, and that we weren't to let her suffer. She had no finite time frame in mind; there were no specific dates that she was aiming for. She was going to live for as long as she could, and then she'd die, but she wasn't trying to make her remaining time conform to one event or another. There was a limit to the activities that she could now do. She recognized that she was becoming battle weary and needed to slow down. As well, she began to wear a pain patch to help her feel more comfortable.

"I just don't have the energy anymore to continue to fight so hard," Margie said. "There's a great fatigue, and it's starting to set in."

She articulated two preeminent goals: to stay up north as much as she could, and to avoid the hospital if possible, relying on me and my personal support workers instead. She wanted to be in the company of those she loved, at home.

Margie then asked Dr. Davis to explain her medical program to the family. She was on a new medication, he said, that would decrease the secretions of bile. She was also on a clear fluid diet, and it was up to me to decide whether to adjust the amount. Suddenly, he stopped.

"I don't think we need to go into all of these details with everybody. I can talk about it with you and Andrea later," he began, but Margie interrupted him.

"Everything is open," she said. "My life is an open book. All I want is for us all to feel free to ask whatever we want," she told Dr. Davis, looking straight at him. "There are no secrets among us now."

We sat in the quiet that followed Margie's words.
The beautiful intensity of the moment overwhelmed us, and
filled the room with a deafening silence. *She's guiding us
along the freeway she's travelling,* I thought. *She's leading
the way.* And there I was — on the inside lane, just where
Margie needed me to be.

ELEVEN

The very next day, Margie and Saul went back up to the cottage, this time with their family. It was a Friday, so that evening they sat down for a dinner to welcome the Sabbath. Margie stood over the Sabbath candles. After she lit them and said the prayer, she turned to her granddaughter, Stephanie, and told her,"You know, this will probably be my last time lighting the candles. From now on, I want you to light them."

When this little girl grows up, wherever she goes, whatever she does — whenever she lights the Sabbath candles, she'll undoubtedly think of her grandmother.

By the time she died, Margie had left each one of us with an experience to remember her by forever.

Finding foods that would agree with Margie became my mission in late August. It was a struggle — Margie was basically limited to clear broth and Jell-O. Every once in a while she could tolerate a little bit of yogurt with some oatmeal, or perhaps some Ensure, but the obstructions were becoming more frequent. We were preparing to handle these episodes at home, but a major one on the 29th of August caught us off guard. We had all the proper medications on hand, but none of the necessary equipment. Soon, Margie's discomfort became unbearable. Sandy stayed up with her through the night, attempting to calm the pain, and Dr. Davis came by to help in the morning. We tried desperately to stay out of hospital, but soon realized that this obstruction had gone on too long to be corralled at home; once again, Margie and I were heading off to the hospital. Dr. Davis informed the emergency department that we were coming, and we prayed that the experience this time would be more compassionate than the last.

Our prayers were answered — the difference between this emergency visit and the previous one was astounding. Margie was admitted immediately. No hand-wringing or humiliating pleading was necessary. The abdominal X-ray confirmed the nature of the obstruction, and without delay, Margie was connected to an IV. A young resident explained to us that the only remedy was another surgical procedure. Without that, the obstructions would eventually lead to Margie's death. His voice was full of care and concern for Margie, and for her condition.

"It's the only thing we can do," he said. "We need to schedule you for surgery."

"I thank you very much," Margie replied, "and I know that the only way to fix this problem is through surgery, but I'm interested in comfort measures now only."

"I'm not sure if you understand," he started again. "Without surgery, you'll die."

"I know I'll die. But what I really want to do now is be with my family."

I sat beside the bed, allowing Margie to explain her philosophy to this young doctor, who was clearly startled by Margie's response, and the composure with which she provided it. Sure enough, the senior doctor entered the room as well, and explained the whole scenario to Margie once again. And once again, she provided the same answer.

"Are you sure that you understand?" he asked.

"You'll die. Doesn't it bother you?"

"What bothers me," she said slowly, "is not that I'm going to die; it's that my husband is outside right now, and I can't hug him."

She was clarifying for the doctors as best she could her judgment that quality of days was not to be sacrificed to quantity. Her decision was so rare, and yet so appropriate. The staff did not know quite how to handle it. After the doctor left, a nurse asked me if Margie knew exactly what she was committing herself to.

"All she wants is to be comfortable," I said. "She just wants to stay here until she's stable, and then she'd like to go home. I know it's unusual, but just think for a moment: you'll never forget this woman. She's got a plan, and she's sticking to it. Look at it as a blessing — you're in the presence of a woman who is actually in control of her death."

The ordeal of this latest obstruction and the rush to the hospital that followed forced me to again confront the possibility that Margie might be unable to fulfill her wish to die at home. Even though Saul had confirmed his support of Margie's plan, the fact remained that he wasn't getting any younger. Sandy and I had more than enough trouble handling the obstruction ourselves, and I shuddered to imagine the fears that Saul might experience were the same thing to happen when he was home alone with Margie. We filled out applications for palliative care at both Baycrest and Princess Margaret Hospitals, mainly as a contingency plan. Our mission was unaltered, but Margie understood that as her condition deteriorated, the possibility existed that her goal might prove untenable. While Margie remained in the hospital, I was in constant contact with the Temmy Latner Center, planning with them for the care and equipment that Margie would need upon her return home; we all appreciated that the previous level of care under which we had been operating was no longer sufficient.

Margie's physical struggle continued unabated. She was forced to limit her intake of fluids — nothing felt right in her system any more. She was becoming bloated from the lack of nutrition, and she struggled to maintain the energy necessary to keep that clarity of thought that remained so important to her. Her questions shifted from focusing on her recovery to death itself – she was constantly curious about the dying process. *What would it be like? Would she know when it was happening?* She always spoke about how critical it would be for Saul to be there with her through the end. But the gravity of the situation was becoming more difficult for him to bear. When we brought all of the equipment to their home in preparation for her discharge from the hospital — the IV pole, the suction machine and all the medical supplies — I could tell that the realization that Margie's death was not far off had hit him extremely hard. Margie was released from the hospital on September 3rd, and returned to the makeshift hospital we had created at her house.

That afternoon, Margie called.

"Andrea," she said, "Saul had a stroke."

TWELVE

I shrieked when I heard Margie say those words. I couldn't believe that this was happening. Margie had been looking forward to settling back into her home, and now everything was once again up in the air. Apparently Dr. Davis had come by to see Margie, and noticed that Saul was displaying strange symptoms. He called 911, and an ambulance rushed Saul to the hospital, where it was confirmed that he had suffered a stroke. Margie was now alone, and asked me to come and be with her. She also wanted me to pick up Vivian, her favorite care assistant. I told her that we'd be there as soon as possible.

For the first time, I was without a game plan. All of the difficult circumstances through which we had navigated these last months had been somewhat predictable, and all were understandable. Saul's stroke, however, was completely unexpected, and left me uncertain of how I was going to make sure that the wishes of Margie and her family

were fulfilled. Would she be able to stay at home? Would
Saul be able to come home? There were no answers, only
endless questions.

When we arrived at the house, Margie met us at
the door. We hugged — neither of us knew what else to do.
Finally, Margie spoke.

"I think it would be best for you to go down to the
hospital to be with Saul — to look out for him and to make
sure that he'll be okay. And I'd like Vivian to stay here
with me."

Vivian and I agreed. We knew that we could not
leave Margie alone, but at the same time, someone needed to
be at the hospital to advocate on Saul's behalf. As I rushed
from the house, I assured Margie that I'd check up on her
during the evening.

I acted for Saul just as I had for Margie. I met
with the unit manager and the rest of the stroke team,
and filled them in on the entire situation — that Saul had
been under tremendous stress lately, and that it was very
important that the family, including Margie, be able to visit.
There had been a terrible influenza breakout and they were

keeping all visitors from entering most hospitals. I told them that Margie was very weak, that her time was limited, and that she wanted to be there with Saul if possible. Their response was outstanding. They understood the uniqueness of this situation, and made it clear that they would respect Margie's desire to be with Saul at the hospital. My relationship with the hospital staff now established, I directed my full attention to Saul.

I accompanied him as he underwent a battery of tests, and I related his story to the many specialists on the team who were assessing him. He was feeling terribly guilty — as though his stroke had detracted from Margie's journey. I tried my best to reassure him.

"Just let the guilt go," I advised. "You need to focus on yourself right now — you've got to get your health back. Margie needs you to get better, and then you can be there for her when she needs you."

Saul nodded in agreement. He couldn't help but feel as if he was letting Margie down: she needed him to be strong for her. I just had to continue to tell him that the only way for him to be strong for Margie was for him to first take care of himself.

It was an exhausting, difficult day for Saul: he had navigated from Margie's return home to finding himself right back in the hospital. The stream of tests seemed endless. Through it all, however, Saul and I achieved a new understanding of each other. I had always felt a slight, yet palpable level of apprehension from this man, as though he was quietly uncomfortable with my role in Margie's odyssey. Perhaps it stemmed from the association between me and Margie's fate, obviously a difficult area for him. This silent barrier dissolved through the course of that day, though. He saw me at work, making sense of what was going on, looking out for his specific interests, remaining level-headed in a high-stress environment. Finally, he observed as I made his greatest wish a reality: I arranged with the staff to permit a visit from Margie.

Sandra accompanied her visibly weak mother. Margie's slow movements betrayed her frailty. And yet, she came alive at the sight of Saul. Their eyes locked together in an intense connection.

"I love you," she said.

"I love you, too," he replied.

And then they embraced and the tears began to flow. As they expressed their deep love for each other over and over again, my own emotions began to well up inside of me. Margie was so fragile, and yet she managed to tap into an awesome reserve of strength — of incredible fortitude – in order to say to Saul, *I love you, and I will support you as you have supported me.* I knew she was tired; she was completely fatigued by the multitude of obstructions and the inescapable pain that plagued her. But for this moment of need, Margie transcended her physical limitations, invigorated by the opportunity to help her husband.

During the two days that I spent with Saul at the hospital after his stroke, he began to divulge just how he was coping with his wife's illness. He was resigned to the fact that she was dying — he could sense that the end would arrive very shortly. He reiterated that he was fully supportive of our approach, and of Margie's goal, a gentle death. Even in his compromised situation, he, too, was priming himself for what he knew would be an intense run for us all.

I kept in close contact with Margie during these two challenging days. She had been amazing since Saul's stroke — she truly rose to the occasion. Her decline had begun to accelerate rapidly during the previous week, and while we were at the hospital, she expressed her doubts about whether dying at home would be possible given the strain on Saul. And yet, the opportunity to care for her husband had given her that little boost she was clearly needed. She committed herself to living long enough to see Saul through his recovery; she would be strong as long as he needed her to be.

Behind the attentive and energetic front, though, it was clear that the illness and the added stress were wearing Margie down. On the fifth of September, we met with Dr. Davis, and Margie finally gave vent to the emotions that she had suppressed through the past few days.

"I'm just so tired," she admitted dolefully. "I'm completely wiped. And you know, I don't want to prolong this dying process any longer."

She wanted to help her husband, and then she

wanted to be allowed to die. There was a limit to how far her reserves could be stretched and Margie had almost reached that point of no return.

The doctor suggested that we bring an IV hydration system to the house. He believed that an increase in fluids might provide Margie with the added sustenance she needed to carry her through this intense and stressful period. Margie agreed to it, cautiously; she was slightly wary of anything that she believed would prolong her life unnecessarily. I tried to reconcile her to the IV, using the language that had guided us throughout.

"Margie," I said, "you're still that beautiful flower, but now you need water; you need to be refreshed. Then, you can continue to bloom."

By that afternoon, a community health nurse sent by Dr. Davis had arrived at the house to set up the IV hydration system. Finally, I felt we once again had our hands back on the reins.

argie was visibly reinvigorated by the hydration system. We were preparing for Saul's upcoming return home from the hospital on September 6th, and the fluids seemed to give her the energy to cope with the tension and the anticipation. When Saul returned, Margie insisted on being involved in his care. She dedicated much of her days to spending quiet hours with her husband. Refreshed as she was, she now handled the pressure well, and focused her attention on his recovery — looking after all his meals, safeguarding his rest time, or just ensuring that the care assistants gave him the best attention possible. I recall this interval that Margie and Saul spent so closely together as a precious treasure: she rose above the pain and turmoil to give this most beautiful gift of care to her husband.

Now that Saul was resettling well, I was able to return my attention to Margie. She would express her concerns about Saul's condition to me, and I made sure that I was as positive and uplifting as possible for her. And yet, despite the partial rejuvenation she received from the IV, her own struggles continued to increase. The pains would often come on at night, as she got ready for bed.

"It gets so painful — so sore," she told me. "All I can do is close my eyes and hope it passes."

I informed Dr. Davis of these new symptoms, and he prescribed medications to combat them. Nevertheless, I knew that these pains were only the precursor of what was to come. We were approaching the end.

Once again, Margie's family assembled in the Goldens' living room. Margie had asked her rabbi to join them in order to inform everyone about death and the mourning process, and also to answer any questions that they might have.

After the meeting had concluded and we were once again alone, Margie seemed troubled.

"What's wrong?" I asked. "Would you prefer to have these sorts of meetings privately from now on?"

"No, it's not that, Andrea," she responded.

"We need to do the meetings this way. Everyone needs to feel as if they are part of this experience."

"Are you in any pain?"

"I am, yes — but I'm just trying to get my mind around all that we're talking about. I want the information — all of it. It's just . . . not easy," she explained.

Margie had already accepted her fate. But as time progressed, and meetings such as these became more pertinent, the gravity of what she was accepting sank in. This was her challenge — she refused to disconnect from her own life.

The only member of the family who was excused from our group meeting sessions was Saul. He had attended the first one back when Dr. Davis explained to the family the options facing Margie. But afterward, he told me that it was just too painful for him to deal with; he didn't believe that he would be helpful at the meetings, as the discussions always reached a depth about which he was uncomfortable speaking. Instead, meeting time provided Saul with another opportunity to rest. After the bouts of dizziness that ini-tially had bothered him were resolved, Saul was recovering remarkably well, and the additional rest was putting him firmly on his way to restored health. Nevertheless, the entire situation at the house was very much touch-and-go: Saul was recuperating and Margie was unwell.

I needed some breaks, too. I was spending great amounts of time at the house in order to help keep things calm and to safeguard against anything that could potentially take us off course. We decided to increase the number of hours of personal support assistance from Vivian, allowing me to step back for some occasional time off, while still maintaining my confidence in our ability to sensibly manage any crises. The increase in support took a great weight off my shoulders. I now felt as though the situation had stabilized and we were no longer forced to improvise. The house was once again a place of calm, and Margie's desire to end her life in her own home seemed again attainable.

FOURTEEN

Not long after Saul had returned home, Margie came to me with a request. She told me that she and Saul had discussed taking one last trip up north — her final time at the lake — and she wanted all her children to come up with her. She knew that it would be a challenge, even for one night, but she felt that, together, we could make this dream come to fruition.

"We'd like you to come with us," Margie said. "And if anything happens, we can always come back down."

I called Dr. Davis for his approval. I told him that I would be with the Goldens, and we'd bring along the IV equipment as well.

"This should be a really nice trip, Andrea," he told me. "I think it's great that she's doing this — and you make sure to have fun, too."

I let the community support service staff up north know about Margie's plans. They had gotten to know

Margie during their occasional visits to see her while she was up at the lake, and they were so pleased to hear that she had chosen to make a final visit to their splendid lake country. Margie set the trip's date for the tenth of September; we had only a few days to prepare.

Margie took it easy for the couple of days preceding the tenth. She needed to save up her energy to savor every moment spent at her favorite place. On the day that we were to leave, the nurse from the public agency came by to disconnect the IV system. She, too, reacted with enthusiasm to our upcoming trip. Positive vibes radiated from all corners as we hit the road in the mid-morning.

The cottage was gorgeous: elegant, yet rustic, situated gracefully by the shores of the lake. The sun was hot and high in the sky. Margie and Saul went in ahead with their kids while I unloaded the car, paying special attention to the IV equipment. As I entered the cottage, Margie emerged from the bedroom, wearing a bathing suit.

"I think I'd like to go for a swim," she said.

We all made our way to the dock. The water was warm and lapped softly against the dock's wooden sides.

I had taken some Saran Wrap from the kitchen, and wrapped it around Margie's arm to cover the port for the IV system. Saul and I sat on the dock, our eyes on Margie, as she slipped slowly into the lake.

At first, she treaded water for a while. And then, as her tentativeness wore off, she began to take a few strokes. She swam somewhat gingerly, careful not to loosen the cellophane covering. But the look on her face was one of sheer joy as she basked in the pleasure of the fresh air, the peaceful water, and the soothing sun beating down on her. Eventually, she swam toward the dock, and climbed back out.

"I really enjoyed that — such a nice swim," she said.

And then, she found an open spot on the dock, knelt down, placed her hands on the warm wood, and executed a headstand! It was the same old Margie, all right. She was suffering — struggling, ill, dying — but her spirit was irrepressible. She was up at the cottage to live life fully, the way she always had, doing the things she could always do — and there was no reason to hold back now.

Margie also wanted one last chance to play hostess.

She had invited a number of her friends from up north over for a dinner party that evening. A local girl came by in the afternoon to assist Margie and their devoted property caretaker with the preparations for the party and to handle the kitchen when the guests were there. By late afternoon, all was in order. When her dear friend, Lydia, stopped by to pay a visit, Margie found another activity for us all.

"Let's give Andrea a tour of the entire property," she suggested. "She's never been here before, and besides, I'd like to take a look around once more myself."

And so we set out for a tour, Margie and Saul, Lydia, and me. We went back down to the lake, and walked around the gardens. All the while, Margie described the numerous memorable events and magical moments that had occurred in each special spot. It was an emotional time for her; this was the last time she would be able to see her beloved lakeside property. She also told me about the cottage itself – when they built it, how it evolved, what made it so unique and precious to her. Perhaps she just needed to make certain that I understood all the facets of her life that gave her happiness, as we embarked together on these final days of her life's voyage.

After our tour was completed, Margie, Saul, and I returned to the cottage. Lydia returned to hers, looking forward to the dinner party that evening. Both Margie and Saul were tiring somewhat, and so as Saul went to lie down for a while, I hooked Margie up to the IV system and engineered some quiet time for her.

Finally, as evening drew near, the guests began to arrive. Saul welcomed them and introduced each to me. We made small talk for a while — *What do you do? Where are you from? Do you have a place nearby?* I spoke again with Lydia, telling her just how much I had enjoyed the day.

"It *was* lovely," agreed Lydia. "I'm so glad that you were able to see Margie as she's always been."

By seven o'clock, all of the guests had arrived. The only person missing was the hostess.

The bedroom door opened, and there she was. Elegant and beaming with a renewed radiance, Margie stood in the doorway wearing an exquisite pant suit, as well as her trademark pink lipstick. As always, her stunning silver hair was pulled straight back in a pony-tail. I had never seen Margie like this before: she owned the room with the power of her presence. She greeted her guests, and then headed to the kitchen. She had a dinner party to put on.

We all sat around the dinner table – that is, all of us except for Margie. She was totally immersed in the kitchen preparations. She oversaw every plate and every dish with an eye to perfection. As much as I would have preferred her to sit down and conserve her energy, I knew how important it was to her to have a night in which she could behave as she always had. Everything was executed so beautifully — from preparation to presentation to taste. Even Margie got to experience the taste a bit: although she was limited to a clear broth, she managed to nibble at little pieces of the food she had prepared, sometimes soaking them in the broth to soften them. She continually turned to me to ask about the different foods — *Can I have a little piece of this? Can I try that?* Everything about this evening was to be an exception from the every day. She even had a little sip of vodka to celebrate her success.

After dinner, the party continued in the living room. Time passed quickly, and at nine o'clock, Margie signaled me from across the room.

"What is it?"

"Come on, let's go," she whispered to me. "Come with me to my room."

I was surprised. "Don't you think you should say good-night to all of these people?" I asked.

"No, I think I just have to leave it like this," Margie replied. "I'm going to go to my room now."

As we walked toward her bedroom, we both glanced out the window. The moon sat high in the sky, and shone with a bright orange glow. The party had moved to the deck; they too were staring at the moon. Thousands of stars hovered over the peaceful lake, magnificently illuminating the boundless black sky.

I had known Margie for eight months already, but I got a different sense of her that night. I saw her in her element: this was her life before circumstances harshly forced her path to cross my own. Margie had exposed this segment of her existence just long enough for me to see it, and then, at the high point of the evening, she drew the curtain. Her friends remained, but Margie had left . . . on her own terms.

I hooked Margie up again to the IV system. She was a little queasy.

"I feel a bit different tonight," she said. "I think it's because I celebrated and had a little taste of the vodka. Maybe it didn't agree with me."

That night was indeed different. There was an unusual lightness about her, and even though she became sick, the feeling didn't dissipate. She did not complain; she did not want to put any kind of negative spin on the evening. I managed to get her nausea and pain under control with the help of medication, and she was in such a beatific space that the time passed with relatively little discomfort. After a few hours, she managed to fall asleep.

I tiptoed out of the bedroom and shut the door behind me. The guests by now were long gone, and the cottage was enveloped in silence. Margie had not seen them come, and she had not seen them go: her final image of the evening was a completely timeless moment of pulsating vitality.

Margie and Saul were already up when I entered the kitchen for breakfast the next morning. We talked about how much we had enjoyed the evening, and how well everything had gone. "I just want to tell you how glad I am that you came up here with us," she told me. "It was such a wonderful day — it's so beautiful up here."

"Would you prefer to stay up here?" I asked.

"You mean to die?" said Margie. She always cut straight to the chase.

"Well," I explained, "you seem to enjoy your time so much here. I could try to arrange things so that you don't have to come back to Toronto, and you could stay at the cottage. It's your call . . ."

Margie cut me off. "No. I know I love it here. I'm so glad we made this trip. And I had such a great time last night. But at the end, I have to be back at home.

100

ANDREA NATHANSON

It's just . . . cozier. It's the right place to be."

I was fully supportive of her decision, but still I wanted to know what was behind it. "How do you mean 'cozier'?" I asked.

"I love it here," Margie said, "but it's just too big. I won't be able to get my mind settled — I'll be too concerned about the place. I'll have too much to worry about. I want to be at home."

Once again, Margie had come to a conclusion with the perfect clarity for which she strove. She thought everything through, and then made the decision on her own, not as a prisoner of circumstance. And she realized that this was a gift.

In the late morning, I started loading up the car for our return to the city. As I carried some bags to the garage, I saw Margie walking toward me with a beach towel.

"Don't worry — you don't have to wrap up my arm," she said. "I'm just going to take a little dip."

She walked down to the dock sat on the edge and dangled her legs in the water. Then she dried off, and prepared to close the cottage for the season, as she did every year in the fall. Their caretaker was there, and she

led him around the property, explaining what she wanted

to send down to the city, what she wanted to keep, and

what she wanted to give away. She again tapped into her

incredible energy reserve as she made sure that everything

was taken care of properly; she didn't want to leave this

job half done. Finally, I informed Margie that it was time

to leave. She lovingly thanked the caretaker for all of his

help and devotion, and made sure that he had noted all of

her instructions before we all got into the car and headed

home. There was no longer any reason for Margie to come

back — her story up north had had its perfect closure.

FALL

FIFTEEN

Back in Toronto, we slipped quickly into our routine. Margie continued with IV hydration during the night. In the morning, she would disconnect, and her day would usually include a trip to the health club at a nearby hotel. She'd do a little stretching, have her hair washed, and sometimes — Saran Wrap covering her arm — she'd even go for a swim. It was good for her to get out, but she would return home totally exhausted. Despite her courageous facade, she was continuing to weaken.

Margie was also beginning to suffer from increased pain and bloating. She was no longer taking much fluid by mouth; even the Jell-O and clear broth were beginning to give her some difficulty. She would try to get water down in order to keep her mouth moist, but sustenance was becoming extremely limited.

Although Saul was still in the early stages of

recovery from his stroke, he decided to try gradually get-ting back to work. Ordinarily, I wouldn't condone such a quick return, but in his case, it was therapeutic. Home was not really a restful place for Saul, representing, as it did, Margie's illness. But Margie continued to keep tabs on his progress. She insisted on being informed about all the details of his recovery, and continued to assist in the preparation of his meals. She was determined to hold on to life until he was settled.

In the middle of September, as Margie's life neared its end, I was now making daily visits to the house, and Margie asked for an official one-on-one meeting with me. She wanted to reassure herself that we were still on track — which I was keeping ahead of the game and ready to handle any trouble that might arise. She brought up our goal once again — a gentle death. She also informed me that she still felt that there was quality to her days, and wanted to continue with our program of pain management and IV hydration.

As Margie's condition became more and more dire, I ensured that Vivian took a central role at the house.

Vivian had gotten to know Margie very well, and was
comfortable working to Margie's high standards in terms
of household cleanliness and order. Margie was a very
particular housekeeper, and Vivian met her expectations
– they were an excellent match.

But when neither Vivian nor I was around, I ran
into trouble. It was unreasonable to expect me to be
present 24/7, and when a problem crystallized that had
been brewing for some time, I decided that now it was my
turn to call a meeting with Margie.

I realized that the relationship between Margie
and me had progressed to such a high level of comfort that
our communication was actually suffering! I was trying so
hard to shield Margie from any worries or uncomfortable
realities that the previously-established open lines of communication were now not as open as they needed to be. In
essence, I recognized that my usefulness to Margie was
dependent on whether or not I was physically and spiritually
charged, and I could feel that my batteries were running
dangerously low. I knew that the next few weeks would
be taxing in both time and energy. By not granting me an

opportunity to exhale and renew my strength, Margie was unwittingly sabotaging her own best interests.

How did it come to this? How could our extraordinary relationship be suddenly reduced to anxious phone calls and frustration? I sought to rectify this gulf of comprehension in our meeting. It was apparent that Margie was completely in the dark as to what *my* needs were – or, more precisely, what *my* needs *for her* were. If the dying process was to be gentle, I had to be in a gentle frame of mind.

No one was going to change Margie at this point in her life – her standards and expectations were more or less set in stone. What could still change was her understanding of me. So I was painfully honest with her. During that conversation, Margie came to understand the pressure that had built up on my shoulders for the last few months, and she began to comprehend that I was not trying to step back and leave her to fend for herself; I was simply withdrawing to gather my reserves so that I could come back in full force.

It was soon thereafter that I promised Margie that I would move into her house when we knew that her death was imminent. I could sense that my help would be essential toward the end. There was only one catch: I would stay until the weekend — but I would then go home for a day.

"That's so wonderful of you, Andrea," Margie said. "It will be so good to have you with me. And I *want* you to take one day to be with your family." The lines of communication were fully open once again.

In the middle of September, Margie took on a new project.

"I'm organizing a big picnic this weekend – I want to see the whole family."

Margie promptly invited her entire extended family to a beautiful park in the city, where they all gathered on a simply gorgeous afternoon while Margie held court. It would have been very easy for her to keep the reality of her failing condition limited to her inner circle of immediate family and dearest friends, but Margie wasn't about to hide from these relatives. Many of them had not seen her recently, but they loved her and were concerned for her.

110

ANDREA NATHANSON

Moreover, they were curious; they wanted to see how she was doing, but didn't want to intrude upon her. Margie decided not to wait; she chose to go out and be with them, revealing herself in all her frailty, but demonstrating a courage unhampered by fear or embarrassment. She knew that she would be gone soon, and that, for many, her death would be extremely difficult. By engaging so many with such selflessness, she sought to make the end pass more kindly.

The night that followed the picnic proved to be one of the most amazing experiences that Margie shared with me. I was asleep at home when I got a call from Margie in the early hours of the morning. She was in pain, and she described it as a deep, burning sensation within. I left for her house immediately.

I found Margie in her bed with Sandra beside her. I gave Margie some medication to calm the pain and relax the spasm that had once again arisen. Eventually, the pain subsided, and Margie began to rest peacefully. But suddenly,

she was wide awake, and seized by an incredible alertness
that froze everything in time. This was her moment, I realized – an episode of intense clarity that I had witnessed in
my patients so many times before. Margie again became
calm, but her extreme awareness was undiminished.

"I feel . . . I'm not inside myself," she said.

"What do you mean?" asked Sandy.

"I'm — I'm looking down on me...and I'm
galloping...I'm riding toward this bright, bright orange —
this orange orb — and it's getting brighter and bigger and
closer."

"How do you feel?" I asked her.

"I feel . . . so free — I'm boundless. I'm galloping
freely to this brightness and it's so beautiful."

Pleasure bathed Margie's face. She was enjoying
her experience beyond herself so much, and she shared it
vividly with us. She saw her mother — and told Sandy not
to worry about her. She would soon be with her mother in
this blissfully beautiful place, and she would be free.

As I watched this awesome combination of peace,
tranquility, and poise descend over Margie, and observed

her comfort her daughter, holding her hand and consoling her in advance with visions of the future, I became convinced that Margie was receiving an otherworldly gift. There was a certainty in Margie's voice that could only come from the incontrovertible presence of truth. Her eight-month-long pilgrimage now had a visible destination.

Margie's experience lasted two whole hours. Sandra and I stayed by her side throughout. We were all emotionally drained by the end, and yet suffused by the pervading sense of an overarching peace.

After the night of Margie's visions, it was clear to me that she had progressed into her life's final stage. The soul was becoming stronger; the body, weaker. Her temporal worries, however, were becoming more severe. The pain would simply not go away. I recognized that we would need to expand the nighttime care in order to quell any painful attacks immediately, and I arranged for a nurse to spend nights at the house, arriving at nine in the evening, and relieved by Vivian at seven the next morning. By now, Margie's greatest fear was not of death, but of pain.

"You promised to make sure that I wouldn't be in

pain," she'd remind me, just to be certain that no one had forgotten her primary goal.

Even when Vivian was at the house during the day, I ensured that Margie always had some medication on hand, just in case an attack occurred while she was at the health club or elsewhere. For a few days, this approach seemed to be working. Then, one morning, Margie called and asked me to come over quickly.

When I arrived, her pain had increased, and she was restless and agitated.

"Oh, Andrea," she said, "I'm in limbo - one foot is here on earth, and the other one has already left this place, and has gone to where I was the other night."

She became increasingly anxious. I was finally able to calm her with pain medication and a mild relaxant. I decided to ask her to describe this state of limbo in which she found herself.

"I just don't feel like I fit in here anymore," she said, as a few salty tears began to trickle down her cheeks. "I go to Starbucks every day, but I can't drink coffee. I just go for the outing. And then I look around, and I see everyone else with a cup, and I realize that I'm becoming an outsider — I feel like a phantom."

She seemed so frail that one strong gust could blow her away.

"I really don't know where I'm supposed to be," she continued. "I know what I have to look forward to, but I can't get there yet — and I can no longer participate in this world. So where am I supposed to be?"

The tears flowed freely now. There was no longer any time or need to repress her feelings.

"You don't have to be anywhere you don't want to be, Margie," I suggested to her. "You're free to go to that place where you're galloping — and you don't have to fight it. And other times — when you want to be here, and live your life here – you don't have to feel guilty about it. There's no "one right way" to go through this part of the passage. You're free from the restraints of both places. This limbo is a kind of freedom."

She listened to me, but she was still confused; the situation was overwhelming. Her body was like a trap, and her soul was continually trying to find its way out.

SIXTEEN

Margie would crawl into bed exhausted, feeling as if each night was the end. By the morning, however, she would wake up fully hydrated.

"Oh my, I'm alive still!" she'd exclaim.

The hydration had restored her, but the morning still left her confused. *Was she dying, or was she not dying?* She felt as if she'd been tricked.

By the third week of September, Margie began to suffer from hunger pains, which continued unabated, since she couldn't eat. She constantly reminded me of the importance of a gentle death, but that quality of death for which we had striven all these months was becoming more and more elusive. Margie was becoming more emotional in the company of friends and family, and spoke about death much more often, with the result that many visits from her loved ones ended in tears on all sides. Margie was no longer willing or able to be that rock, wowing everyone with her poise.

Now, Margie's journey was transforming into a sprint. I desperately tried to slow the pace down, through pain control and hydration, but much of my work seemed to be in vain and every morning seemed to herald an additional calamity. Margie struggled to maintain some semblance of a life in the midst of her visible decline, but I could see that the level of control we had established was slipping away.

Retrenchment came about after a visit from Dr. Davis. He believed that we were not on a downhill course, but rather, a plateau. True, her pain was increasing, but the IV hydration allowed her to continue living with a reasonable amount of energy. When I explained to the doctor how I felt we were sprinting toward the finish line, he gave us a different perspective and some advice. "The way I see it," he said, "this is more of a marathon than a sprint. She's not on her deathbed," he said, fixing me with his gaze. "Maybe you should just slow things down, and give her some space."

He also suggested that people not hover around Margie so much. Morning, noon, and night, Margie's children had been stopping over and tearfully saying their final good-byes. Then, the next day, they would repeat the whole process again; Margie had lived another day. We realized that the constant reenactment of Margie's farewell was counterproductive and depressing for everyone. Moreover, it appeared panicky, and perceptions mattered. So I set about trying to maintain a continuity of caregivers, to increase the sense of tranquility within the house. The meeting with Dr. Davis gave us renewed purpose, and some peace of mind.

I was at the Golden house on the 25th of September when Margie suffered another obstruction. We decided to treat the situation at home, rather than submit ourselves to the delay of a trip to the hospital. I gave her the medication to relax her body. However, Margie no longer had the strength to recover her energy alone. I hooked her up to the IV hydration system, and she went to sleep. When visitors came, she roused herself, but she lay asleep for much of the day. In the late afternoon, Margie woke up and announced, "I'd like to call my doctor, please."

"You mean Dr. Davis?" I asked, moving toward the telephone.

"No," she said. "My doctor."

She meant her long-serving family physician. He made a house call that evening. Although I had never delved too deeply into Margie's relationship with this doctor, I knew she considered him a confidant. The fact that she had called for him suggested that she sought to discuss something beyond the routine. I sensed that Margie was preparing to make an important decision.

"All along, I've looked to retain the quality in my days," she said to him. "Now, it's no longer there." Though she tried to discuss options with him, they both knew that there were only two. Finally, she made her decision. She could no longer justify prolonging her life. She wanted to stop the hydration. She would rest and then let nature take its course.

I never think it wise to make major life-and-death decisions at night, or when under some acute attack, and

I told this to Margie. She agreed to continue with the hydration that night, and reevaluate in the clear light of morning. I was certainly not against her decision – the gentle journey she had hoped for was becoming obscured by pain and medicated haze — but I wanted to ensure that she was one hundred percent certain of her choice as well.

I entered Margie's room late that night. Sandra was already there, lying beside her mother on the bed, talking and cuddling. Margie motioned for me to come over to the bed, and I sat in a chair by its side. We talked through the night. Margie spoke about her decision. She knew what she wanted to do, but wanted to make sure that her decision was informed by the clarity she had desired back in January.

"I can no longer say that I have any quality of life," she told us. "What else is there to do?"

The next morning, Margie reaffirmed her decision to put an end to the hydration. I spoke to Saul later that day. In the wake of Margie's decision, we were all faced with the realization that Margie's death was now breathing down our necks. Saul knew that I had made tentative arrangements with a few palliative care hospitals in case Margie's aim, a death at home, proved unattainable. I decided to put the question to him: did he feel comfortable with his wife's wish? Was he capable, physically and emotionally, of handling her death in their home?

"Well, I *have* been thinking about it," he said slowly, even cautiously.

I had no idea which way he would go. I knew that his heart would be with his wife's goal, but his condition in the aftermath of the stroke could tip him in the other direction.

"I want Marjorie to stay at home," Saul said self-assuredly. "I know I can handle it."

It was not an *"I guess, if she has to"* sort of concession. To Saul, this was not just what *she* wanted; it was what *he* wanted, too. His wish was a beautiful act of love.

Margie had a close relative in the Baycrest Nursing Home. The lady was not in strong condition, and it had been Margie's plan to make one final visit to see her. But as time went on, and Margie grew weaker and weaker, the possibility of a visit became more and more tenuous. The biggest impediment was the NG (nasogastric) tube: Margie did not want to leave the house with the tube in place. Margie finally resigned herself to the impracticality of the outing. This was one plan that she had to let go.

Fortuitously, she did not have to let go for long. On the night of September 28th, the NG tube came out by itself. She didn't feel nauseous or uncomfortable without the tube, and we realized that this was the perfect opportunity to make that final visit.   The outing also presented me with the opportunity to prepare her home for the final stage.

That family visit was the last excursion Margie took.

The hospital bed sat right in the middle of the living room. I did not want Margie to die in her bedroom, which was a sanctuary that needed to remain a place of comfort for Saul. Margie agreed with me fully on that point, so, while she was at Baycrest, I had had a hospital bed delivered to the house and set up in her living room.

"Let's move it right here," said Margie on her return. "Let's put the head beneath the painting."

I wheeled the bed over toward the wall and positioned it as Margie had requested. Then I looked up at the painting. It was of a staircase — a staircase without an end. The steps rose from an indeterminate blackness, and as they climbed higher, they steadily ascended into a golden light before disappearing into the brightness entirely.

The light itself was the destination, and it was under this painting that Margie chose to end her journey — that is, the part of her journey that we could see.

Her own climb out of the darkness had begun with those first few bold steps off the plane from Houston under her own power. Our nine-month journey together had taken her from a winter of despair, through a spring of hope, and a flourishing summer of renewal. And now what? Soon she would know. She trusted in the beneficence of her destination – in its gentleness, its tranquility, and its liberation. But first, she had to experience her own physical autumn.

As we were walking out of the living room, Margie

stopped me. "Let's talk about how I want the room set up,"
she said.

And so she mapped it all out for me: how she wanted candles placed all around; where I was to set the family photographs; what type of music she wished to play. She also requested fragrant flowers to surround her. She then proceeded to her bedroom, and slept through the manicure and pedicure she'd arranged. She wanted to keep any outward trappings of death far away from her.

While she slept, I prepared the living room to her specifications: scented candles, flowers, photographs, gentle music softly playing. And when she awoke, I took her to see my handiwork.

"How do you like it?" I asked her.

"I feel proud," she said, a smile crossing her face.

We sat and talked for a long time. She described the sense of peace that enveloped her, and spoke of the colors that seemed to be hovering around her. We discussed maintaining that feeling — how to accept the warmth and calm that had descended upon her, and how to relax into it. She was experiencing a great change, and she needed to teach herself how to come to terms with it. She lay down on the hospital bed, fatigued, but before I left the room, she grabbed my hand.

"I need to dictate something to you," she said. "I want you to write something down for me tonight."

I agreed to do so later in the evening. And, as I left the room, I turned back to take in the sight of what we had done in that space: the bed, the painting, the candles and flowers — and the nail polish. *Why, this was like a deathbed scene in some grand drama,* I thought. *And I had a central role!* As always, Margie had staged it. She had written the final act in the play of her own life.

SEVENTEEN

That evening, I returned to take Margie's dictation. Just as on the night of Margie's visions, Sandra was lying alongside her mother.

"I need to tell you something, Andrea," said Margie, "and you need to write it down. It's a message that I have to leave behind; I have to give this to Sandy's kids."

The dictation lasted forty-five minutes. Her thoughts came to her slowly and methodically, but what emerged left me stunned by both its power and brazen honesty. As she spoke, she kept her right hand firmly fixed upon her left breast. These were her words:

In my arms I caress you —
Each one of you, each time.
The burden disappears, and I begin to fly;
My soul takes off — Oh, how weightless! How pure!
And then I breathe again.
IN — OUT.
IN — OUT.
I am one with the air — I am my breath;
I am everywhere.
SMILE!

I am there.
Of my life, I only see my love.
I tried it, and I still feel it.
My arms open up; a great goodness rushes in.
It is the gift of love —
Oh, Oh my God! It descends upon me!
It descends in a burst of radiance – in a burst of light!
Love is the light; and I feel it is good.
One day, you will see this light – this burst.
It is as deep as the earth, as wide as the sea, as bright as the
sun,
And it engulfs me.
Oh God, it engulfs me; it guides me home.

As I wrote down the words, I watched the expressions on Margie's face. Physically, she was weak, and yet the depth of the passion painted on her features was remarkable. Her spirit was strengthening — it was transcending her body. Her voyage of discovery was over; she had successfully reached its end. All that was left was the final transition.

That evening I moved into the Golden home, and the four nights that I spent there were a whirlwind. I did not sleep during the entire time — there was always someone to see, or something to do, and, as planned, I was Margie's surrogate: I spoke for her when she was no longer able to do so. Sometimes, I'd lie down on the couch for a few moments, just to recuperate in the most marginal of ways, only to be roused by another task. I threw myself fully into this spectacular cauldron of emotion and passion, of life and death. I don't know whether I could ever do it the same way again, but at the time, I gave myself no other option. It was something that I, personally, had to do.

The stream of visitors was endless; all wanted one last chance to see Margie — their mother, grandmother, aunt, cousin, and friend. Generally, someone would arrive while another was still visiting. I'd sit the new arrivals down in another room, and they'd reveal how much Margie meant to them, what kind of experiences they'd had together, and how they were coping with the end of Margie's life. I saw how this woman's example had changed a whole family — everyone felt free to express themselves because she had told them, *"there are no secrets among us now."* So each one would enter the living room to spend some final, memorable moments with Margie, I ensured that the visits were not too long or intense; Margie was on medication to allow her to descend into a peaceful sleep. She had to rest in order to let herself go.

Margie was in and out of consciousness — awake, then asleep; an alert gaze, then a vacant stare. She would fall into a beautiful zone of peace, and I could sense that she was dreaming. Oftentimes, she would cry softly before waking up, only to realize that she was still alive. She thought she had died; she thought she was in heaven. I would also spend time alone with her — just talking. We spoke about the weather: she loved the rain, and delighted in the brilliance of the lightning that illuminated the sky. We often also talked about the road she had chosen. I told her how courageous she had been — how brave it was to be so involved in the end of one's own life, and in choreographing a gentle death. Perhaps she had not beaten the objective odds of survival, but she had survived in a different way: she had successfully charted her own course. The disease had dictated the terms, but she never let it map the route.

On the afternoon of October 1st, Margie awoke from a nap, took in her surroundings, and appeared content. "It's just so beautiful — so pure and so loving," she said. Then, as I fluffed her pillow, she turned to me.

"Andrea," she said, "I thank you from the bottom of my heart."

She put her head down to go back to sleep, but then added, "And always remember to be nice."

EIGHTEEN

Margie became increasingly unresponsive during the days that followed. Sometimes she'd rouse when she could sense the presence of a visitor who was very dear to her, or whom she had not yet seen. She stirred when the rest of Sandy's family arrived from Utah, and she always rallied when Saul entered the room. He would try to soothe her with gentle words or permission to let go, but she never could when he was around — she wanted to be with him. I suggested to Saul that he try to get out of the house sometimes, to get a bite for lunch or to go for a walk, both for the fresh air and to let Margie descend back into tranquility. I promised to call him if there were any sudden changes in his wife's condition.

Margie was fully at ease when she was alone with Sandra and me. There was no standing on ceremony — amongst the three of us, everything had been said.

And so, in the early morning of the third of October, Sandy and I sat by Margie's bed, each holding one of her hands, chatting about my background, and Sandy's early years, her relationship with her mother, and her life in Utah. And we talked about how much we had learned and grown as we had travelled this path with Margie. Margie, meanwhile, did not rouse at all. She lay peacefully in her bed, comfortable in her surroundings and her company.

The third of October was a Friday. I had originally intended to go home that afternoon, assuming it more than likely that Margie would not still be alive. But although she was by now largely uncommunicative, she was still very much with us: her pulse was strong and her body was warm. Dr. Davis had come by the house, and had advised us to take Margie off much of her medication, as the end was near. In the late evening, when Vivian arrived to spend the night with Margie, I left the Golden house for the first time in four days, and went home.

I was quite certain that I would not be with her as Margie took her last breaths. And in hindsight, that's the way it had to be. I had done my job: for nine months I had

ANDREA NATHANSON

managed to keep Margie's journey on track. Her lucidity was unimpaired and she appreciated the tranquility that enveloped her progress. Her final triumph, in a sense, was that she could die without me. She was with her family, and she felt safe and secure. In that sense, she had beaten the odds. Now it was time for me to return to *my* family.

I arrived home a little before ten o'clock that night. My husband and children were still out at a Friday night dinner, and I headed immediately for the shower. I stood under the water for nearly an hour, slowly decompressing from the intensity of the past week. Eventually, I heard the front door open as my family returned. I let out a sigh of relief. It was good to be back.

The next morning I called Vivian at the house. The night had gone well: she had cleaned Margie's face and combed her hair, and Margie had remained calm through the night. The nurse from the government agency had already arrived, and Vivian gave her a thorough report, bringing her up to speed on how to manage Margie's care through the day. She was confident that Margie's comfort would be properly maintained until the end.

At midday, I called to see how Margie was doing. Sandra told me that it looked as if the end was very near.

"It's so hard to watch her as she goes through this," she said.

I reminded her that Margie would soon be where she had traveled to on that memorable night, and remarked on how marvellous it was that her mother's efforts and desires had been realized: her path had followed a seasonal cycle: she had bloomed, and it was only natural now that she would fade. It would be difficult to watch, but it was natural. "Just remember," I told her, "Margie's going where she wants to be. A chapter will close today, but she will soon be galloping freely, just as she described to us."

At 2:25, no more than twenty minutes later, the phone rang. Margie had passed away.

I was emotionally distraught, but managed to pull myself together and drive down to the house. The doctor had not yet arrived, but he soon joined us, and after he made the pronouncement, we called the funeral home to make the arrangements.

I stood in the living room with Margie's family — Saul, her children, and her grandchildren. Subconsciously we positioned ourselves around Margie, until we formed a circle surrounding her. Suddenly, Saul began to speak. He told us their story — how he met Margie, fell in love, and how he introduced her to his family. He described their early years together, and as he spoke, we instinctively grabbed for each other's hands. Our circle was connected all the way around, and a lovely harmony filled the room.

When the people from the funeral home arrived to take Margie away, the reality of her death hit home for many of the family members, and they burst into tears. For my part, however, I looked up at the painting on the wall, at the head of the bed. I had guided Margie up the staircase, but the final step was hers to take alone, and now she had. She had entered that great light at the top of the stairs. Her soul was free.

Following the funeral and the week of mourning, many weeks passed before I spoke to the Goldens again. I knew it had to be that way. We all had to get on with our lives *after* Margie.

But within a few months, we began to speak again. Saul and I have maintained a friendship, and I've coordinated his care for many years since. I've watched him re-establish his life not just as a widower, but as a survivor. I've also connected with family members who were at more of a remove from Margie. They've all commented on the newfound sense of strength that they noticed in Margie at the end of her life, and the courage, joy and settled mind that she displayed. Many marvelled at the bond that Margie and I built, and were inspired by the faith that carried Margie through her illness. Her life touched them all very deeply and profoundly.

Many paths converged with Margie's journey. I still reflect on my own learning and growth, and of the intellectual leaps taken by Saul, Sandra, and so many others to reconcile the course that Margie chose with their own wishes and preconceptions.

In total, there were forty-four people who assisted Margie on her journey, and I like to think how profoundly she might have impacted those travellers on life's road as well. I suspect many of them, when called upon to offer words of comfort or wisdom will begin, *I remember a silver-haired lady who, when confronted by death, instead chose life.*